FATHERS, FLYERS & THE MOST INFURIATING MAN ON EARTH

by Julia Woods

What could my father have been *thinking?* To buy me a birthday present of flying lessons of all things! Not only does he know that I'm petrified of flying, but who does he hire as my instructor? Brawny daredevil Ethan Ross, who enjoys risking life and limb—just for the fun of it! I prefer to live my life catastrophe-free, thank you very much. It's clear that both our fathers, who have been best friends for fifty years, have a hankering to become in-laws and decided to play matchmaker with us. Well, I can't imagine spending more than five minutes with a fearless Ethan without wanting to run for cover, much less imagine ever becoming his lawfully wedded wife! Sure, the thought of being in a cramped plane with this powerful, potent man gives me an adrenaline rush and makes my heart do palpitations. But if he thinks he's got the upper hand, he's in for the shock of his life...!

∧∧∧∧∧∧∧∧∧∧∧∧∧∧

❧ FAMILY ❧

ᴧᴧᴧᴧᴧᴧᴧᴧᴧᴧ
⚘FAMILY⚘

Helen R. MYERS

A Fine Arrangement

Make me a Match

Published by Silhouette Books
America's Publisher of Contemporary Romance

SILHOUETTE BOOKS
300 East 42nd St.,
New York, N. Y. 10017

ISBN 0-373-82153-0

A FINE ARRANGEMENT

Dear Reader,

Matchmaking can be fun...when it's happening to someone else. The instant it's your own family that has taken up the cause as their new recreational hobby, it can be annoying, embarrassing and just plain bad on the nerves.

That's what happened to Julia and Ethan, as their war-buddy fathers prove how strategy—regardless of whether it's militarily inspired or born of wistfulness and love—is, er, imperfect.

In the end, Woody and Harlan do get their way. So do Ethan and Julia, although they needed some time to realize that. Of course, just to keep things interesting not all goes as planned.

If you have a family of your own, you know exactly what to expect. All that remains for me is to wish that *your* dreams come true.

Always,

Helen R. Myers

Please address questions and book requests to:
Silhouette Reader Service
U.S.: 3010 Walden Ave., P.O. Box 1325, Buffalo, NY 14269
Canadian: P.O. Box 609, Fort Erie, Ont. L2A 5X3

For my brother, Robert C. Renko,
who made Flying 101 without a
dimenhydrinate bearable, and for my sister-in-law,
Beth, his adventurous Camcorder operator

Prologue

"You know, there comes a time in a man's life when his daughter's birthdays become downright depressing events," Carl "Woody" Woods said, breaking the silence that had ruled for the last fifteen minutes of the poker game.

On the other side of the scarred, but solid, table, his longtime friend, Harlan Ross, lifted his bushy, reddish-brown eyebrows. "Julia having a birthday again?"

"Time flies."

"What's this number, twenty-seven?"

"Twenty-eight."

"Jeez."

Woody sighed his agreement and inspected the

five cards Harlan had just dealt him. They did nothing to change his morose disposition. "I'm beginning to think she's going to live with me forever."

"I feel the same way about Ethan," Harlan said, adding consolingly, "but at least your Julia's a good cook. Last night that boy of mine made meat loaf, and I swear I still feel like I got one of his airplane tires rolling around in my gut." He discarded four of his cards and flashed his friend his ace keeper, before reaching for the deck and issuing himself four new ones. "Thirty-three years old, and he's still as wild as a mustang."

"Remember when there used to be a natural order to things? You and me, we understood it. We came back from Korea and got married, had the kids...we knew our responsibility."

Harlan rubbed his aching belly before reaching for his beer mug. "For a while there I thought Lola Higgins might catch his fancy. It was clever of her to sign up for flying lessons just to get close to him."

"Her only mistake was getting airsick," Woody said with a philosophical shrug.

"Losing her temper with him wasn't a good move, either. A woman interested in a serious relationship with Ethan would have to appreciate his diversified talents and understand that he's usually got more than one thing on his mind at a time. Could he help it if he forgot he wasn't stunt flying for a few moments and did that rollover?'' Grimacing, Harlan gestured at Woody's cards. ''You gonna discard or what?''

Woody shifted in his chair and adjusted his glasses. ''I guess I could keep these.''

Though Harlan grumbled about being set up, they played out the hand. Afterward, Woody scooped his winnings, a pile of unshelled peanuts, into his dish. As he took out two and began to crack them open, Harlan reshuffled the deck.

''So,'' he asked, ''what're you getting Julia this year?''

''I don't know.... Do you suppose there's such a thing as a mail-order groom?''

Harlan made a tsking sound in sympathy. ''I'd have thought Vern Culpepper would have popped the question by now. They've been keeping fairly steady company for—why, it's been several years, hasn't it?''

Woody dismissed that with a shrug. ''I guess. But Julia treats him like he was her brother, and as far as I can tell, Vern isn't in any hurry to figure that out. Not that it matters, though. Never did want him for a son-in-law, anyway. His TV commercials are stupid.''

''Too bad she and Ethan don't get along. You could try giving *her* flying lessons.'' In a feeble attempt to hide his appreciation of his own wit, Harlan ducked his head to hide his grin as he shoved the deck of cards across the table to his friend.

Instead of cutting the deck, Woody just sat there and stared at him.

Harlan finally looked up and, seeing the other man's expression, rolled his eyes. "It was a joke."

"No, wait a minute. You might have something there."

"Woody...out of respect for over fifty years of friendship, I'm going to try to say this delicately. Julia isn't exactly the type to catch Ethan's eye— even if they could stand each other, which you know full well they can't. Now don't go getting all puffed up," he added soothingly, as his friend went ramrod straight in his chair. "It isn't that she's not attractive in her own way."

Woody thrust out his chin until he almost had one. "Allow me to remind you, *old friend,* that Ethan wouldn't win any beauty contests himself."

"It's the hazards of his professions," Harlan said, quick to defend his son. He gestured with his palms upward. "As a part-time crop duster, part-time stunt pilot and part-time flying instructor, he's in the air more than he's on the ground. It's inevitable for him to have a scratch or two. Why, I sort of look upon them scars and busted bones as medals, you know? Okay," he mumbled, lowering his eyes from

Woody's unblinking scrutiny. "Maybe not all of those stunts worked out the way he expected, but the important thing is that he's walked away from most of those mishaps under his own steam."

"Most of those mishaps have occurred in the past two years. Maybe Somebody's trying to tell him something." Woody reached out and divided the deck in half, his expression indicating that he was satisfied by how he'd gotten Harlan on the defensive. "Now you take my Julia. She's got a good head for business. Ethan could do a lot worse. I'll bet she could even point him in a new direction...at least he wouldn't have to keep worrying that one day his nose was gonna resemble a head of cauliflower."

A glimmer of interest lighted Harlan's eyes. He ignored the cut cards and, resting his elbows on the table, leaned toward his friend. "She did real well for you when you wanted to trade in your old station wagon for a truck at Oscar's dealership, didn't she?"

"By the time she finished pointing out the infractions of the city building code in his showroom, he was ready to improve his trade-in offer by three hundred dollars," Woody replied, his chest thrust forward in pride.

Harlan nodded thoughtfully. "Come to think of it, she has a real nice voice, too—when she ain't lecturing. Why, they never ask anyone else to sing a solo at the church Christmas service, do they?''

''And you'll remember that she always makes extra biscuits on Saturdays, because she knows you're going to show up and drool into my plate,'' Woody added to tip the scales further in his favor.

Rubbing his mouth, Harlan thoughtfully eyed his friend. ''You're putting ideas in my head, Woody, old boy. Hot damn, I'm getting an idea.'' He narrowed his eyes speculatively. ''The question is, would we still be welcome for Saturday breakfasts once she and Ethan were hitched?''

''Why, it would only be fair, considering all we'd have done for them.''

That was enough for Harlan to start collecting the cards and shove them back into their box. ''Come on, we gotta go,'' he said, rising.

''Where to?''

''The airport. I think you should take a look at the nice gift certificates Ethan's got for those lessons we talked about.''

Woody eagerly pushed himself to his feet. ''Do you suppose I could get one in pink, Harl? Julia's real partial to pink.''

Chapter One

If she wasn't a lady, she would have been tempted
to say something vile. But as Julia Woods glared at
the receiver in her hand, she acknowledged that old
habits were hard to break, and took what consolation
she could in *thinking* of a few choice words she
would have liked to recite to the person she'd been
talking to, instead of actually saying them. Maybe
one didn't get off scot-free for doing that, either—
she'd once had a long talk with the Reverend Mr.
Neely about such things—but considering her cur-
rent state of mind, not to mention the ringing in her
ear, she would argue with anyone that the milder
infraction was justified.

Men, she fumed, slamming her own receiver onto

its cradle. Heaven save her from the lot of them...including her father...but most especially Ethan Ross. Her right ear was still reacting to the way he'd just hung up on her. If she went deaf from this, he was going to hear a lot more from her than her opinion of Ross Aviation's *company policies*.

What an uncivilized cur. No refunds on gift certificates, indeed. Who did he think he was? More important, what was she going to do if she couldn't change his mind? As she grew aware of the curious stares she was receiving from the other employees at city hall, Julia self-consciously fingered the bun at the back of her head. She had to collect herself. It would not do for people to see the municipal clerk of Gator Cove giving in to emotional outbursts, she reminded herself.

Straightening her spine, she glanced down at her half-eaten sandwich. Ordinarily she liked pimiento cheese, but there was no way she was going to be able to finish the sandwich now. She was simply too upset.

This was all her father's fault—at least indirectly. What in the world had possessed him to buy her a gift certificate for flying lessons for her birthday— or, for that matter, anytime? He knew she loathed flying. More accurately, she was *terrified* of flying. The very thought made her stomach queasy and had her once again wiping damp palms on the skirt of her dove-gray, shirtwaist dress.

No, her father wouldn't have done this to her. But she knew who was undoubtedly to blame. Harlan Ross. He and her father had been friends since they were boys. They'd even gone through the Korean War together—though Julia was certain her father's survival had been nothing short of miraculous, since Harlan was, and always would be, a bad influence on Carl Woods. Hadn't history proved that whenever her father got into trouble, it was invariably due to some bright idea Harlan had come up with? In such cases, wasn't the first sentence out of her father's mouth usually, "But Harlan thought..."? That was the trouble; Harlan schemed, but it was her father who was left to explain the ensuing calamities.

And, of course, Harlan was Ethan's father. That explained a great deal. This father and son pair gave new meaning to the term "chip off the old block." Both Rosses were big, brawny men. Their hair was forever in need of combing and cuts, its unusual shade of reddish brown adding amber light to whiskey-brown eyes. And those eyes held enough of a devilish gleam without the help.

In fact, as far as she could tell, there was only one significant difference between the men. Unlike his father, who whiled away his days at Rocky's Bar and Grill—Gator Cove's less than commendable answer to a community center—and plotted how to get everyone else into trouble, Ethan's brainstorms only involved himself. Julia wasn't sure the distinction was anything for the younger Ross to gloat over, because most of his ideas were dangerous.

When he wasn't playing dive-bomber or crop dusting area farms in his grasshopper-green plane, he was testing the laws of aerodynamics by trying to satisfy some ambitious Hollywood director's desire for a memorable movie stunt. Julia wouldn't deny the man had talent—he'd lived to be thirty-three, hadn't he? But she was also sure that some of his less successful landings—not all of them had been *with* the plane—had loosened his brain in the process. If he enjoyed his work, that was fine with her, but it didn't mean she was going to get into a plane with him. Therein lay her problem.

Ethan's third job, the one she calculated he worked at the least, was as a flying instructor. And her father had already paid for her lessons in full. Cash that Ethan had just told her was nonrefundable, due to some idiotic policy he'd probably made up while they'd been talking on the phone.

Well, her father might be a soft touch where the Ross men were concerned, Julia fumed, as she came to a decision and rewrapped what was left of her sandwich, but she wasn't. She was going to go out to the airport and settle this thing, once and for all.

"Bobbie Lee." She took her purse out of the bottom drawer of her desk and crossed over to the vivacious brunette. Bobbie Lee Cobb collected city water payments, opened new accounts and served as receptionist in the building, when she wasn't devouring movie-star magazines or flirting with whoever walked through the front door. "Would you please take my calls? I have to leave for a while."

Bobbie Lee touched a finely manicured hand to her impressive bosom. "Make my day, Julia. Tell me you've actually decided to go *out* to lunch. Better yet, tell me there's a gorgeous new guy in town and he's taking you."

Julia's answering smile was dry. "I know you were listening to my phone conversation. Did it sound like I was planning a date?"

"No. It sounded like you were warning someone to either get out of town or load his six-shooter. But you know me, hon. My great ambition is to die a wealthy optimist." Resting an elbow on the counter, she leaned closer and lowered her voice to a conspiratorial whisper. "Tell me the truth, Julia.... Did your daddy *really* buy you flying lessons for your birthday?"

"Oh, Bobbie Lee..."

"Can I help it if I have twenty-twenty hearing?

Anyway, I think it's sweet. And if you ask me, you're a lucky woman to have the opportunity to spend all those quality hours in one itsy-bitsy plane with a big, strapping man like Ethan Ross.''

Julia could feel twin spots of color stain her cheeks, but she forced herself to resettle her glasses on the bridge of her nose and meet the taller woman's dreamy eyes. ''And I think you should be institutionalized. Do you ever think of anything besides men and—men?''

''Contaminate my mind? No way.'' She grinned at Julia's pained expression and maternalistically straightened the pristine white bow at her co-worker's throat, until Julia impatiently brushed her hands away. ''Okay, Miss Killjoy. Go on out there and ruin a perfect opportunity, if you must. Only try to remember that you get more bees with honey than with vinegar.''

Julia firmly tucked her purse under her arm. ''I'm *not* looking to start a colony, Bobbie Lee.''

''No kidding,'' Bobbie Lee muttered under her breath. She sighed as she watched Julia leave. ''Sugar, unless you let me get my hands on your wardrobe and that hair, there isn't a drone this side of the equator who'd risk getting frostbite with you.''

Ethan Ross tried to remind himself that generally speaking, he had a great fondness for women. He liked the way they were built. He liked the way they smelled. He even liked it when they pretended to be the weaker sex, though experience had taught him that they were anything but. What he didn't like was a woman who ignored her best attributes and tried to bully him. He *didn't* like Julia Woods.

"Ow—damn!" he growled as his wrench slipped on a nut he'd been tightening and jammed into his thumb.

He backed out from the engine canopy of his dust cropper and brought his sore thumb to his chest, holding it as protectively as a mother would hold an infant. He'd just had the cast on his left arm removed two days ago, and the arm was still sore, not to mention bruised-looking. Now he had another ache to add to the rest.

With another expletive he tossed the wrench into the chest-high toolbox a few feet away and sat down on the plane's sturdy wing. He might not be the luckiest man in the world when it came to safety records, but it sure wasn't like him to be the clumsiest. He knew he had someone else to thank for taking his mind off his work, and that someone was Miss Holier-than-Thou Woods.

Face it, he told himself, carefully massaging his hand. *She's managed to get into your tough, Texas hide again, and she did it as easily as nut grass burrs get into a pup's paw. But what's got you really riled is knowing that you can't afford to shake her loose this time.*

He must have been crazy to accept Woody's money in the first place. Julia Woods flying. Hell, if she wanted to do that, all she had to do was climb onto her broom. If that didn't work, she could always open her mouth, because there was enough hot air spewing from it to launch the Goodyear blimp. No way did she need him. Unfortunately he needed her. Rather, he needed the money he could only keep if she took those lessons.

Ethan scowled down at his injured hand and thought of the accident that might have turned out much worse. For almost fifteen years he'd been doing aerial stunts for films and air shows, and he would be among the first to admit there was always a degree of fear that was logical, even healthy, when doing that kind of flying. But he had never been as afraid as he'd been this last time. Though he'd always known this day would come, he hadn't anticipated the inconvenient timing. The fact was, he'd lost his edge, his attraction for the work, and financially it couldn't be happening at a worse moment.

So much for thinking his work was safely diversified, he thought, shifting to rest his sore arm on a raised knee. He raked his other hand through his hair. He'd once thought that between the crop-dusting business, the occasional movie work and his instruction school, he could make a decent living, even build up a nice nest egg to guarantee him a comfortable retirement someday. What he hadn't counted on was only being thirty-three when he discovered he could no longer stomach doing stunts.

And who could have foreseen that he would develop a keen interest in environmental protection so that he would end up worrying about the detrimental effects of crop dusting? He glanced at the solidly built plane that had brought him so many hours of flying enjoyment and felt the familiar tug of nostalgia.

All he would have left once he let it be known that he was out of the crop-dusting business was his school for flying. But in the small, Texas coastal town of Gator Cove there weren't many people who were anxious to soar among the sea gulls. Even fewer who could afford to pay for the experience.

He didn't think for a minute, however, that he was down for the count. If he knew one thing about himself, Ethan knew he was a survivor. He had exciting plans for the future. But those plans were going to take time and more money than he'd been able to save. That was why, no matter how strongly he was tempted, he wasn't going to give Julia a refund.

For a fleeting moment humor got the best of him, and the hint of a smile tugged at his lips. Truth be known, he was actually looking forward to getting Miss Prim and Proper into the cockpit of his Cessna. With her schoolmarm's bun and those big glasses that gave her a bookish, disapproving look, she gave the impression that nothing could rattle her. After knowing her for most of her twenty-however-many years, he wanted the chance to try.

"Ah, Woody," he sighed, gazing out the opened doors of his hanger at the empty runway. "I don't know why you really got her that certificate, but I could kiss you for it."

Just as he was about to take a break and hunt down something for lunch, Ethan saw a compact Chevy pulling in beside his Jeep. He didn't need to peer through the windshield to identify its occupant—the vehicle's bland, beige color alone put a grim smile onto his lips.

There would more likely be pansies growing in Hades before Julia Woods drove or wore anything that wasn't as colorless as she was herself. As she emerged from the car, Ethan took in the gray, shirt-waist dress with its white trim at the cuffs, its high collar and starched bow and almost laughed. She was one of a kind, all right. Even in a pitch-black room he knew he would be able to identify the skinny-minny. Her sharp little nose would poke him right in the Adam's apple, and he would have to fight his way through a handful of hairpins if he ever wanted to explore the texture of her hair.

Explore? Ethan shook his head and pushed himself to his feet. Maybe his blood-sugar level was low. It would be a long day coming before he would want to explore anything about this prim woman, who, he suspected, had starch running in her veins.

"Well, well, Miss Julia," he drawled, intentionally using one of the nicknames he knew annoyed her. "Why am I not surprised to see you?"

"Common sense, Ethan," Julia replied, tucking her purse under her arm with the military precision of a cavalry officer positioning a riding crop. "When you slam down the phone on someone in the middle of a conversation, you have to expect a response."

"Were we in the middle of a conversation? I thought you'd said what you had to say. I know I did."

Julia seethed. How she despised his lazy drawl and careless walk. Who did he think he was, dressing in that black T-shirt and rumpled jeans, some fifties movie idol? Well, he might look threatening with those muscle-bound shoulders, ham-hock forearms and carved granite face, but she knew what was really beneath that mussed head of flame-tipped hair: Dennis the Menace, who'd never grown up.

"I know this is going to come as a revelation to you, Ethan, but I haven't said all I had to say."

Stopping only two feet away from her, he hooked his uninjured thumb in one of the belt loops on his jeans and gave her a sardonic smile. "Have at it, honey...only be warned that you're wasting your breath. Not that you don't have extra to spare."

Her mouth already open, Julia closed it with a snap. Exhaling in frustration, she pushed her sliding glasses up her nose and glared at him. She had to remind herself that she didn't approve of violence, because she really was tempted to reach up and punch him in his crooked nose. Never did it occur to her to be intimidated by those brown-gold eyes, deep set beneath his broad, jutting brow.

"What is it going to take for you to understand that I don't want those lessons? Even if I did, I wouldn't take them from you!"

"Shh—" He raised his throbbing hand to his lips and pretended to look around. "Are you forgetting your daddy and mine have been friends since they were knee-high renegades? It would break their hearts to learn you and I couldn't get along long enough to get through a few flying lessons together."

"You know perfectly well that my father is keeping your father company at Mrs. Van Rosenbeck's bar—*as usual*."

Ethan ignored the intended jab. Just as they would never be friends, they would never agree on which of their fathers was the worse influence when it came to spending all that time at Rocky's. He had other arguments to win today. "No refund, Julia."

He turned away from her and headed toward his office. She followed, barely suppressing the desire to grab his arm and swing him around; of course, she knew she would have more luck trying to move that hideous green plane.

"But if I refuse to take the lessons, you'll *have* to give me back the money."

"Nope."

"Of course you will. Services not rendered. There's a law or something that says so."

Ethan opened the glass door to his cubbyhole of an office and stepped inside, confident that Julia was right behind him. When he pushed aside a stack of papers on his desk and sat down, he found himself almost eye to eye with her. It gave him a funny feeling, as if he were looking into the face of a small, wary owl. That was what her soft, gray eyes reminded him of behind those damned glasses. He liked owls. There was one that nested in his hangar. What he didn't like was discovering that Julia reminded him of one.

"Your father gave me permission to wait you out."

"He *what?* What do you mean, 'wait me out'?"

"Wait until you decide you'd like to start the lessons. Or wait," he added with a devilish grin, "until you succumb to my persuasive charms."

Julia pursed her lips and tapped her left foot. "Have you just come out of the hospital from transplant surgery? Imagine...and me not even aware you'd been out of town."

"The mouse needs longer legs if she'd going to kick dirt in the lion's face," Ethan replied, giving her a Cheshire-cat smile.

He was no lion, he was a big ape who was single-handedly driving her crazy. "Look, Ethan, either my father was under the influence or he lost some ridiculous bet to your father during one of their marathon poker games. Whichever the case, he couldn't have been in control of all his faculties."

Ethan shook his head, negating the idea. "I made him touch his nose with alternate hands and walk that white line out on the runway."

Julia was not amused. "Why would he *do* this to me?" she moaned, rubbing the spot between her eyes that was beginning to throb.

"Has it crossed your mind that maybe he simply wanted to do something nice for your birthday?"

"He could have given me the money he gave you, and I could have bought new drapes for the house. That's what I would call doing something 'nice.'"

"Drapes..." Ethan let his gaze drift from her fine, brown hair to what seemed to him almost child-sized feet clad in conservative, gray pumps. "Mouse, you need a transplant yourself if you think new drapes are what'll put pizzazz in your life."

"I didn't say anything about 'pizzazz,' and I don't need any advice from *you*. What's more, I'd appreciate it if you would once and for all stop calling me *Mouse!*"

Ethan lifted both of his eyebrows and crossed his arms, an action that seemed to test the sturdy fibers holding together his T-shirt. Things, he decided, were getting interesting. If Julia could be counted on for one thing, it was her even temper. As a child she'd been more of an adult than Woody, undoubtedly compelled to fill in for the woman they'd both lost too early in their lives; and even as the ever-efficient municipal clerk at city hall, she could be counted on to keep things running smoothly, no matter what the crisis. But she was losing it now, and it made him wonder why.

"Miss Julia," he drawled in that lazy way he knew could make her compress her unpainted lips. "Could it be that the notion of being in a cramped Cessna with me makes you nervous? Are you afraid that maybe my bare arm will touch yours, and I'll mistakenly think you're coming on to me? Or maybe if your knee accidentally bumps my thigh,

I'll experience such a rush of uncontrollable passion, I might not be able to keep myself from doing this...." With a speed that defied his size, he reached out and grabbed her waist, jerking her forward until she was nestled between his thighs and half sprawled against his chest.

Julia didn't have time to do more than gasp. The assault sent her glasses sliding down to the tip of her nose. But she couldn't be bothered with them. She was too busy trying to brace her hands against his rock-hard chest. Of all the crude, insufferable people, she fumed. Why on earth did their fathers have to be such great friends? And *why* did Harlan have to have had *him* for a son?

Then Julia felt her glasses slip the last centimeter and tumble off her nose completely. It didn't hamper her vision at all, not at this close proximity. But suddenly, as her gaze locked with Ethan's, she felt the air in the cramped, musty room grow thin and entirely too hot. When his gaze dropped to her lips, she felt her own eyes grow wide in horror. With a gulping sound that could have been a hiccup or a groan, Julia jerked out of his arms.

Ethan told himself he was relieved. It had been a bad move. A woman like Julia could get the wrong idea from a situation like this. Anyway, it had been disturbing—no, annoying—to have her so close that he was made aware of the scent of her flowery-sweet bath soap. Even now it lingered, though he was trying to purge it from his lungs.

"Calm down," he muttered, irritated further by the way she was gawking at him. Reminding himself that it just might be because she was myopic, he glanced down to see that her glasses were balanced on his thigh. With a promise to have a long talk with his own father for helping to get him into this mess, he thrust them back at her. "You didn't think I was serious, did you?"

"Of course not." Julia paused to slip on her glasses. After taking a steadying breath, she cast him a wary glance. "You weren't, were you?"

"Are you kidding?" He burst into laughter, though the moment he saw her offended look, he tried to squelch it and gestured reassuringly. "Sorry. It's not that I—well, you have to admit the idea of you and me...that we... Well, it is pretty bizarre."

Julia lifted her chin. "Indubitably. The mere notion that I could be attracted to a man who dates women with cotton candy for brains is as outrageous as it is insulting."

"Hey, wait a minute." Ethan shifted his hands to his hips. "Vern Culpepper is no Einstein."

"I never said he was, and if you're suggesting he and I date, you're wrong. Vern and I are merely friends who enjoy each other's company. As for his intelligence, his success as a businessman speaks for itself. You, on the other hand, are an adolescent in a man's body who, considering your insane choice of profession, undoubtedly suffers from a death wish!''

"Thank you all to hell," he growled. "I suppose I should be grateful you even noticed the body."

How could she miss it, when he dressed like that? Julia thought waspishly, dropping her gaze to her clasped hands. She wasn't handling this well at all. Why did she always find herself on the defensive with this man? Why did she feel she always had to prove something to him? She was behaving no differently than she had when she was eight and would ride her bike to town on an errand and he, already overconfident at thirteen, would snatch her change purse from her basket, teasing her until she was red-faced with fury and close to bursting into tears.

"I'm sorry," she said, her tone formally conciliatory. "I've never approved of people who base their arguments on personal attacks. I'm even less tolerant when I sink to that level myself. But Ethan, you must see how impossible this whole situation is."

He shrugged and then nodded, almost tempted to apologize himself. It hadn't been nice to laugh at her. She might be somewhat prim for his taste, but she wasn't all that bad-looking. If she ever loosened up enough to let down her hair, both figuratively and literally, she might even be cute. Sort of, he amended, inwardly shaking his head at himself. Had he really thought *cute?* Maybe he'd better recheck the fuel lines on that crop duster; could be there was a leak and he was reacting to escaping fumes.

"Then we can call this off?"

That cleared his mind faster than a phone call from his accountant. Ethan shook his head. "Can't do it, Julia."

"You don't have to give me the money," she pleaded. "Give it to my father."

"I can't give it to either of you, because I need it."

"Oh." It was hardly the answer she'd expected. She sat down, all the fight drained out of her. You could argue with orneriness, and you could debate with stubbornness, but how did one challenge need? "I didn't know things were that bad. I mean, I know you've been out of work since you broke your arm, but—" Belatedly she remembered her manners. "It looks like it's still painful. How does it feel?"

"Better. Good," he amended, flexing it and finding that his thumb no longer throbbed—at least not any worse than the rest of the arm. "I've taken up both planes with no problems."

"Then you'll be able to go back to work soon."

"In a manner of speaking. I'm able to work now, but I'm quitting the movie business."

He might as well have said he was going to shave off all his hair. Julia stared at him, unsure if she'd heard him correctly. "You're giving up stunt flying? But Harlan's always saying it's the most lucrative of your jobs. Crop dusting is seasonal, and as for the flight school—"

"I know how well the school's been received, thanks," he snapped. In three years he'd had a whopping two students who'd completed the course and obtained their pilot's licenses. Even in a town of Gator Cove's modest size, that wasn't saying much. "Anyway, I've decided that it's time to leave the daredevil stuff to the younger guys."

The Reverend Mr. Neely said that miracles still happened in this day and age, but this was one Julia wouldn't have believed, if she hadn't been hearing it firsthand. Still, she knew if she'd been the one coming in for a landing, only to discover that half her landing gear was missing, *she* would have re-evaluated her outlook on life, too.

"You're not that old," she murmured.

Ethan shot her a droll look. If that was her idea of a peace offering, she needed more than flying lessons.

"What are you going to do?" she added, when he failed to reply.

He hesitated, then shrugged. Why not tell her? It wouldn't hurt for word to start getting around.

"I'm thinking of starting an aerial tour service for the tourists who come down to Galveston and Corpus Christi. Give them, I don't know, thirty minutes to an hour of flight time. Let them see the coastline from a different perspective. Maybe fly them out to some of the oil rigs in the Gulf. I want to do the same thing with the businessmen who come down for investment purposes. The big corporations have their own aircraft, but these smaller companies are at the mercy of whatever's available. I want to fill that gap, before too many other people figure out the same thing."

"Won't you need a larger plane?"

"Congratulations. Now you're catching on."

Yes, Julia was. But as she did, she knew she couldn't allow Ethan's plans to interfere with her own, no matter if she *was* somewhat intrigued and admittedly impressed. She shifted her purse, gripping it tightly between her hands. "Ethan, I'll admit that what I know about airplanes wouldn't equal the sand in an egg timer, but I'm fairly certain that my lessons wouldn't buy you more than a couple of tanks of fuel...maybe a decent-sized ad in the yellow pages."

His answering look was determined. "Every dollar helps buy me time to figure out a way to get that plane."

She didn't like the look in his eyes, and definitely

didn't like that answer. Rising, she laid a calming hand to her stomach, willing the butterflies to cease and desist. "That's all very commendable, I'm sure. But it brings us back to the point that I don't *want* to learn how to fly!"

"Why not?"

"Because!" She spun away from him, afraid he would see the fear in her eyes. She'd only been in a plane once in her life, but it had been an experience she would never forget—one she had no intention of repeating. But she would rather let Ethan think what he would before admitting it.

"What's the matter, Mouse? Scared?"

Julia whirled around and gave him a narrow-eyed look. "Of course not!"

"So?"

It was just like old times. He would taunt her, trying to get her to do something she didn't want to, and she would run away. She was tired of it. She was tired of him laughing at her.

"So—so when do we start?" she heard herself blurt out.

He never even paused to blink. "How about right now?"

Chapter Two

Julia had to swallow twice to dislodge her heart from her throat. Brilliant tactic, she silently chided herself. She should have known better than to react so impulsively; after all, when had she ever been successful at bluffing anyone?

Now. The man wanted to start her lessons now, and he knew perfectly well she had no reason not to take him up on it. She couldn't even use the excuse of having a short lunch break. Being the one employee at city hall who *never* took breaks or went out for lunch, no one would ever say a word if, just once, she took some extra time. Because everyone in Gator Cove knew most of everyone else's business, Ethan would be aware of that, too. "What's the matter, Miss Julia? Got a sudden case of cold feet?''

One of these days, she promised herself, one of these days she would figure out a way to wipe that smirk off his face—permanently. She met his twinkling eyes coolly. ''Of course not. I was only concerned that I might be taking you away from some appointment you might have.''

''That's mighty thoughtful of you. But as it happens, I'm all yours.''

Julia ignored the sarcasm beneath those words and nibbled on her lower lip. She supposed it wouldn't hurt to get this over with. The first lesson probably wouldn't be so bad. At least she wouldn't have to worry about actually going *up* in a plane. Since she was a beginner, he probably wouldn't let her do more than fill out some forms and look at a few books. She could tolerate that easily enough.

''All right,'' she said, gesturing around the room that, except for the desk, executive chair and files, contained no other furnishings. ''But where do you expect me to sit?''

''Sit?''

''Down...so you can begin instructing me.''

''Ah.'' A slow grin spread over his face and laughter lighted his eyes anew. ''That's not quite how we do it.'' He crooked his finger. ''Come with me.''

He led her out of the office and through the hangar, back outside, where the already warm May sun baked down upon the packed earth and spring-green grass. Gator Cove's municipal airport was small by anyone's standards, and as a result, only the main runway had the luxury of being paved. Though it had rained two days ago, Julia grimaced at the dust that quickly covered her shoes, and she was relieved when they stepped onto the lush grass beside the hangar. But even that didn't stop her from wondering where he was taking her.

They went around the side of the building where two planes were parked. One, she knew, was Ethan's stunt plane, a fire-engine-red biplane that looked like something out of the silent-picture era. Just about everyone in town had been victimized by Ethan's pranks from that plane. He would dive over their houses or chase their pets and livestock as he supposedly *practiced* his maneuvers. Julia herself had phoned the police department to complain about him on more than one occasion.

The other plane was a smaller, white model with a single, high wing. It appeared put together with nothing more than toothpicks and tissue paper, like those toys children bought at five-and-dime stores. Julia's anxiety grew in leaps and bounds as Ethan led her to it.

"This is a Cessna 150, what we call a trainer,

because it's the most uncomplicated to learn for beginners. This is what you'll be using."

That's what you think. Julia cast him a sidelong look before walking up to the plane to peer inside.

There were two seats, but even so she couldn't imagine more than one person at a time in it—at least not without getting claustrophobic. The seats were plastic, cracked and torn, exposing foam stuffing that was stained with age and grime. The whole thing looked as if it could use a ruthless scrubbing with a liberal dose of disinfectant soap.

Inwardly shaking her head and thinking that in some ways men were all alike, she averted her gaze from the dirty floorboards and considered the dash. It didn't look all that different from one in a car, except that there were more gauges and what looked like two steering wheels. She thought it was clever of the designer to allow a beginner to feel they were actually participating in the flying. But all those gauges...

"I should warn you that I'm not very mechanically inclined," she told Ethan. "In fact, I do well to remember to keep track of the gas gauge in my car."

"You'll learn. All you have to remember is that the propeller isn't going to turn without fuel, and if it isn't turning, you aren't going to stay up there." He pointed skyward with his thumb.

Julia felt her eyes drawn upward and experienced an unpleasant queasiness in her stomach. She took a deep breath, assuring herself that it wasn't as bad as he suggested; he was obviously trying to intimidate her. "It's rather small, isn't it?"

"Yeah, well, I couldn't get a 747 in a color I liked, so I had to settle for this."

"There's no need to be sarcastic."

Instead of replying, he circled the plane and opened the door to retrieve a booklet from inside. It, too, looked well-worn. Reaching over, he pushed the passenger door open and beckoned her to step closer. "This is your preflight checklist. You never, ever take off without running through it. Inside this kit you'll also find your aircraft registration and airworthiness certificate."

"If it's certified as airworthy, why do you have to go through a checklist?"

He stared at her for several, long seconds. "Because," he said slowly, "we have a saying among us. 'There are old pilots and there are bold pilots. But there no old, bold pilots.' Understand?" He waited for her to nod before continuing.

He ran through several more instructions, most of which she missed because she was still bristling from his reprimand. They seemed useless to her, anyway. She would no more leave an ignition switch on than she would leave her car running when she parked it to go into a store. Common-sense things, that was all a checklist was for. She was more than glad to withdraw her head from the musty-smelling plane when he told her they were ready to check the fuselage.

Once again she was subjected to an endless lecture about what one was supposed to examine—things such as vertical stabilizers, ailerons, flaps.... He had her crouch to check the bottom of the plane—fuselage, he kept calling it—for any signs of cracks or suspicious-looking fluid dripping out. Julia inwardly shook her head. If a person was going to worry about a plane being in that bad a shape, why in the world bother to get into one?

"Now you're ready to check your fuel tanks," Ethan told her, stepping to the root of the wing. "Hold on to the wing. Put your right foot on this tab," he said, pointing to a small, metal strip attached to the side of the fuselage. Then he pointed to another step on the wing strut. "And put your left foot here and hoist yourself up. You'll find a fuel cap up there. Unscrew it and—"

"Wait a minute. Why can't I just check the gas gauge?"

"Fuel gauge," he said, with a patience he didn't feel. "Because you can't rely on it. Gauges can be off or even broken." But watching her glance down at her dress, which was already billowing in the light breeze, Ethan understood the real reason behind her hesitation. "Oh, hell. Climb up there, woman. It's not as though I've never seen a pair of bloomers before."

Julia could feel her cheeks singe with the heat of embarrassment. The man was a pig. Someone should have run him out of town a long time ago. But if he thought she was going to let him get under her skin so easily, he had another guess coming.

Without sparing him a glance, she did as he'd directed, gingerly hoisting herself up. However, she couldn't quite help wishing she'd worn her newer slip—the pink one with the French lace. At least she could have proved she wasn't the dull prude he obviously thought she was.

Ethan couldn't help noticing her slim ankles and shapely calves. He's always thought of her as a skinny-minny, but sometime in the last ten years or so Julia had obviously grown up.

He cleared his throat and told her what to look for. After she replaced the cap and climbed down, he pulled out a small, plastic cup he'd retrieved from the inside of the plane. "Next you want to check for any sign of debris or water in the lines." He showed her how to get a sample. "It should be a clear, light blue like this. Watch for bubbles, which means water. When we're having a particularly wet season, you have to be careful about that."

Slightly annoyed that he hadn't complimented her grit, if not her performance with the fuel tanks, Julia muttered, "I wouldn't have to be careful if the manufacturer would build a solid, well-sealed plane to begin with."

"Check the door hinges," Ethan continued through clenched teeth. "Check the vents for bird nests, and check the propeller to make sure there aren't any major nicks." After showing her how to inspect the oil level, he gestured to the cabin. "All right, get in. No, not this side," he said, grabbing her arm and drawing her back when she reached for the passenger's door. "That side."

"Excuse me. I didn't know this was a European-built plane."

"It's American, and the pilot sits on the left side. That's you. The instructor's on the right. That's me."

Though she hadn't expected a student to actually *sit* in the plane during the first lesson, Julia decided to be a good sport about it. After all, the sooner they finished, the sooner she could leave.

She circled the plane and awkwardly climbed in, tucking her full skirt beneath her as best she could. There was no telling what had been dropped on the floor. Just as she'd expected, it was a tight fit inside. When Ethan climbed in beside her, the atmosphere grew absolutely suffocating.

His muscular arm rubbed against hers, the sun-bleached hairs tickling her skin. There was hardly enough room for his long, powerful legs, and his left thigh blatantly rubbed against hers. The only way they could have been closer was if they'd been on a dance floor, or in...

"Now you're up to the Before Starting Engine checklist," he said, breaking into her thoughts.

"There certainly are a lot of checklists," she replied, staring straight ahead at the Day-Glo-orange wind sock near the runway. As she clasped her purse in her lap, her palms grew moist and it wasn't only because of the heat. Don't be an old prune, she silently scolded herself. So she was in close confines with the man; this was no more personal than being examined by a doctor.

"We're getting to the less tedious stuff now," he told her. "This is your throttle. It controls the engine speed."

"Doesn't the gas pedal do that?"

"There's no gas pedal, only brakes, and they're on top of the rudder pedals. The rudder," he explained testily when he saw her blank look, "is that little movable section I showed you on the tail."

"You needn't get snappy. I can't be expected to remember everything at once, you know. What's this?" she asked, pointing to the lever beside the throttle.

"The mixture control. It controls the ratio of air and fuel going into the engine. Now here's your airspeed indicator gauge. You'll have to pay particular attention to that and your altitude indicator. When...*if* you ever get far enough to go for your instrument-rating certificate, you'll learn more about that."

He went on and on until he'd covered every gauge on the dashboard and Julia was thoroughly confused. But when she glanced at her watch, she saw that only ten minutes had elapsed. Even so, she was ready to get out of this sardine can.

"Well, it's been very interesting," she began, reaching for the door handle.

"Fasten your seat belt and make sure your door's closed properly."

She shot him a startled look. "Pardon me?"

He ignored her by securing his own belt and slamming shut his door. "Now remember, before you turn on the ignition, you want to warn anyone who might be standing near the propeller to clear the area. So you open your side window and yell out 'Clear.' Got it?"

She wasn't going to bother asking him why they needed to do that, when it was obvious no one was out there. There were more important questions to have answered. "We're going to actually start the plane?"

"It's the only way I know to get it in the air."

"But I don't want to get it in the air. I only agreed to take the first lesson."

"And this is part of it. Now fasten your seat belt, secure the door and give the Clear signal." When she didn't budge, Ethan gave her an exasperated look. "All right, *now* what's the matter?"

"I'm not ready. You have no business taking an unprepared person up there."

"It's not like I'm asking you to fly the damned thing yourself!"

"There's no call to swear at me!"

There was every call, Ethan thought, raking his hand through his hair. She was single-handedly driving him nuts. If he had half a brain, he'd throw her out of the Cessna and give Woody his money back. But as appealing as the idea was, he knew he couldn't bring himself to do it. He wanted this new business venture too much to be thwarted by one high-strung woman.

"Julia," he said, after taking a calming breath. "I apologize for my language, and I assure you that I wasn't about to jeopardize your safety. I sure as hell wasn't going to jeopardize mine. But in order for you to get a feel for how it handles and how all these gauges work, we need to take it up."

"I really have to get back to work."

"We won't be gone fifteen minutes."

"I don't remember a fraction of the instructions you've given me, as it is."

"No problem. I'll be repeating them again and again until you do remember them. Ready?"

No, she wasn't ready, she was terrified. And what if they crashed? She had a car payment due this week. Her father had an appointment to have his teeth cleaned next Monday. Who would take care of all those little things if she wasn't around to do them?

"Look, if you're too chicken to do this—"

Julia slammed the door, and the plane shook with the reverberating impact. Tight-lipped, she secured her seat belt. If there was one thing she couldn't tolerate, it was Ethan Ross accusing her of being a scaredy-cat. Next he would be teasing her in public, and it was difficult enough to maintain one's dignity in a town where your father was known as one of the two resident clowns. Jerking the window open, she barked out, "Clear! Now what?" she growled at Ethan.

He ducked his head and, to hide his amusement, pretended to scratch an itch at the tip of his nose. When Julia exhibited a little spunk, she was almost fun to be around. "Now we turn on the master switch and key the ignition," he replied, pointing to each for her.

As she turned the key, the engine immediately

sputtered to life. The noise was deafening—to Julia it was like riding a running lawn mower in the garage—and the plane vibrated in protest for several seconds before the engine smoothed out.

"We're going to taxi to the runway now, so put your feet on the rudder pedals!" Ethan shouted.

"What?"

"Your feet." He pointed. "Put them on the pedals!"

"Uh-uh."

"Damn it, Julia. We're not going to go through this every time I give you a direction. I'm going to get us up in the air, but you're going to learn how to taxi this."

Ever since she'd gotten into the plane, Julia had been careful not to touch the pedals on the floor. Though her ankles were cramping from the exertion, she was still hesitant as she lowered her feet. Expecting an immediate reaction, she was as much confused as relieved when nothing happened. "I think it's broken."

"You have to push in the throttle." He pointed to the black knob on the panel. "No!" he shouted a second later when she pounded at the knob with her palm.

Too late. The engine roared like a protesting beast, and the plane leaped forward as if to escape its manhandling. Julia screamed and slammed her left foot to the floor, desperately trying to make the plane stop. Instead the Cessna went into a sharp, left turn. White-faced, Ethan groped for the throttle and pulled it back to the Idle position.

For several seconds, as the engine calmed, he sat there and waited for the death grip his abdominal muscles had on his stomach to relax. "Never," he croaked, "but never do that again. When I said push it in, I didn't mean *all* the way or immediately. Do it slowly, like this, and only until the plane starts to roll."

As the plane eased forward, Julia's eyes widened to a new horror. They were headed directly for Ethan's stunt plane! "We're going to crash!"

"You damn well better not. Depress your right rudder pedal to turn to the right. *Slowly.*"

Julia did as he directed, though not as smoothly as either of them would have liked, and the plane shifted away from the stunt plane, rolled off the grass and bounced onto the dirt road. Delighted with herself, Julia laughed and depressed the left rudder pedal until they made a complete, three-hundred-and-sixty-degree turn.

"Oh, this is almost fun!"

Ethan took his sunglasses out of his T-shirt pocket and put them on, hoping everyone at the other hangars had decided to take a midday siesta, had gone to lunch or was otherwise preoccupied. Maybe he wasn't the most civic-minded citizen in the community, but he had a certain reputation as a pilot. At the rate Julia was going, however, she was going to wipe *that* out by the time they landed. *If* they landed.

He pointed down the road toward the runway. "The idea is to go in a straight line."

That was harder to do than Julia had anticipated, and after several trips into the ditches on either side of the dirt road, she cast Ethan an apologetic look. "I think I'm getting the hang of it."

Rather than answer, Ethan glanced back at his hangar, wondering if he might be leaving it for the last time. *And people said men were more apt to have lead feet?* He exhaled with relief as they bounced onto the pavement. "Okay, now we have to call the airport office and advise them that we're going to take off. The thing to remember is that there are two types of airports, controlled and uncontrolled. A controlled airport is nothing more than one that has a manned tower. If the controller goes home at sundown, it becomes uncontrolled. Basically that's what we have here, and ordinarily there's not as much red tape to go through in take-offs and landings, but our office is pretty good about keeping tabs on things, so we'll let them know what we're up to."

"Excuse me, but I'm hearing only every other word you're saying!" Julia shouted.

"You'll get used to the noise. Just try to pay attention." Ethan picked up the mouthpiece of the radio and keyed it. "Gator Cove Unicom, Cessna Seven Seven Three Five Alpha is departing, Runway Two."

"Three Five Alpha, Gator Tower. Roger, buddy. Where're you off to, Ethan?"

Before Ethan could respond, Julia snatched the mike out of his hands and keyed it. "Kenny?" she shouted above the noise. "Kenny Spivet, is that you? Why, I didn't know you were working at the airport. This is Julia! Julia Woods!"

There was a momentary hesitation and Ethan groaned inwardly as he imagined what was going on at the main office. He had a feeling it would be a while before the boys stopped ribbing him.

"How-do, Julia!"

"What?"

"I said, what're you doing out here?"

"Oh. My father gave me these flying lessons for my birthday—not that that's what I wanted, mind you."

Ethan snatched the mike out of her hand. "Let's get something straight right here and now," he growled, using the ache in his left hand to feed his anger.

"What?"

"This isn't a telephone!" he roared, shaking the mike under her nose. "You want to have a coffee klatch, you do it on your own time, not mine. From now on, when you're in one of my planes, your priorities are as follows—aviate, navigate and communicate. Notice, please, that chatting on the radio comes last on the list. You're to remember that *you're* in control of this plane and not the controller. If he says something to you and you're up to your elbows in trying to control your plane, you take care of the plane first. Your responsibility is to make sure everything goes well with this flight."

Julia lowered her eyes in chagrin. He might be right, but no one had been so short-tempered with her since she was a child. If he wanted to get technical about it, she wasn't actually in complete control of the plane, and she couldn't resist telling him so, adding, "And I can't help it if I was raised to answer a question when I'm asked one."

Ethan muttered something explicit to that and taxied the Cessna onto the runway.

As Julia became increasingly aware of what was about to happen, she felt her stomach grow more unsettled and her skin more clammy. It was so hot, and there was barely enough air to breathe. "Isn't there an air conditioner in this thing?"

"This isn't a limousine."

Oh, dear. Enough was enough. If she didn't call this off right away, she was going to become violently ill, she just knew it. But the moment she turned toward Ethan and saw the little bag he thrust at her, saw the smug expression on his face, she knew she wasn't going to give him the satisfaction of being right about her. Shoving her purse into the pocket on the door, she reached for the bow at her throat and tugged it loose. Then she released the top two buttons of her dress. It didn't provide complete relief, but she figured that at this point every little bit helped.

Admiration didn't come easily to Ethan, but he grudgingly had to admit her response was a surprise. As she wrestled with the collar of her dress, he found himself staring at her hands. He'd never noticed how fine-boned they were...how, even agitated, the slender fingers moved gracefully. She had a real lady's hands, and her skin...it was so fair and smooth, especially at her long, slender throat.

He shook himself from his ill-timed and unwelcome thoughts and snatched up the checklist again. Because he was both disturbed and annoyed to have noticed her as a woman, he was gruffer to her than before. "Now pay attention," he snapped as he lined up on the runway's center line. "You're ready to do the preflight run-up."

He ran through them, hardly caring if she was

paying attention or not. At this point she couldn't possibly want this over with more than he did. Maybe he would reconsider refunding her money, after all. He definitely would, if she got sick in his plane. It would be best to be done with her.

But fifteen minutes later as Ethan landed the Cessna and taxied back to the Ross Aviation hangar, he discovered that he wasn't through with her yet. She hadn't become ill, and except for accidentally sending them into a nosedive when she'd tried to retrieve the pins falling out of her hair, she hadn't really done a bad job when he'd let her fly the plane.

After parking the Cessna and logging her time in a book, he presented it to her. "This is yours. You bring it every time you come here, and every minute you spend in the air gets logged like this." Now, he thought, now she'll tell me that she won't be back. It was the only reason he didn't explain that the timekeeping was their way of telling when she would be ready for her first solo and when she would be ready for a cross-country flight. Since there probably wouldn't be a next time, there was no sense in going into all that detail.

"Wh-when should I be here for my n-next lesson?"

Ethan had begun to turn away and froze. Slowly, turning back, he scowled at her. Damn her for continuing to be such a surprise, and damn her for the

oddly appealing picture she made, standing there
with her hair falling from its bun. The shade wasn't
a mousy brown at all. When the sun shone on it, it
had an understated, ash color that was exactly right
against the creamy skin he'd noticed before. Except
for the twin spots of color in her cheeks, she looked
even paler than when they'd first taken off.

Creamy skin?

"Hell," he muttered under his breath. "Be here
Saturday. Ten sharp."

"Fine. I'll see you Saturday then."

Pushing her slipping glasses back up her nose,
Julia tucked her purse and log book under her arm
and headed for her car. Secretly thrilled with her
achievement, she walked proudly, with her head
high and her shoulders back. At least, she walked
as proudly as her wobbling legs would allow.

Chapter Three

Julia knew she couldn't return to city hall looking as she did, so she made a detour and headed for home to freshen up. Like the Rosses, she and her father lived on the outskirts of town in a quaint, wood frame house Julia had convinced her father to have aluminum-sided several years back. He still complained that people described its color as something between "formaldehyde and frog," but Julia loved the cozy cottage and was proud of the diligent attention she paid to the yard and interior.

All in all she was content with her lot in life, unlike her older brother, who'd wanted more and moved away to seek it. Last she heard, he was a stockbroker in Saint Louis. Except for Christmas cards and birthday cards, she rarely heard from him. It was his opinion that they didn't have much in common. Maybe not. She didn't need fancy cars and vacation homes to fulfill her. In fact, except for having someone of her own to love, she didn't know how else she could improve on her life. But thanks to her father, perhaps there wasn't going to be a life to improve upon.

Brooding on that, she virtually ignored the cascading white spirea bushes and the lingering blossoms on the mountain pinks as she turned into the gravel-covered driveway. But her attention sharpened considerably when she spotted the two-tone-blue pickup truck parked in the drive. It was her father's. Finding him home meant she had that much less time to wait before she could give him another piece of her mind for getting her into this fix. Her resolve revitalized, she parked beside the truck.

"Dad?" she called as she emerged from her car and hurried up the concrete walkway running parallel to the house. She leaped up the four steps leading to the kitchen door and pulled it open. "Dad!"

"Well, so much for my other surprise. Happy birthday again, dear."

She froze midway into the room and stared at the pink and white cake set in the middle of the kitchen table. It wasn't necessary to count to know there were twenty-eight miniature candles stuck on top and that he'd succeeded in lighting only half; nor did she bother reading the pink writing on the top of the cake. She knew it was for her, just as she knew she should be touched by the gesture. But it had been fifteen years since her father had remembered things such as cakes with candles, and it only served to intensify the nagging suspicion Julia had experienced ever since he'd presented her with that gift certificate this morning.

"All right, what's going on?" she demanded of the small, spare man with thinning hair and bifocal glasses who stood hovering over the confection, a burned-out match in his hand.

Woody gave her a wide-eyed, befuddled look before breaking into an overbright smile. "Surprised you, eh? I know you usually bake both of our cakes, but I thought this might be a nice change. Especially since you didn't seem as excited as I'd hoped you would be about your present. Er, are you all right, dear? You look somewhat—"

"Go ahead and say it, Dad," Julia said dryly. "The word you're looking for is *windblown*. Under the circumstances I'm surprised I don't look a lot worse."

"I take it you went to talk to Ethan."

"I thought I could persuade him to give me a refund."

"Good grief, Julia. Tell me you didn't actually get physical with the man?"

Sparing him a droll look, she crossed the room to set her purse and the log book Ethan had given her on the table. "Very funny. I look like this because I had my first lesson."

Relief and delight played across Woody's face. "Why, that's wonderful! Here...sit down. Have a piece of cake. I was just going to get this ready and put it in the refrigerator for tonight, but when I heard your car in the driveway, I couldn't resist. Come on, sit and tell me all about it. Uh—maybe you'd better blow out these candles first. They're melting faster than I thought they would."

Julia did blow them out, but didn't sit down. "There isn't time to talk right now. I have to freshen up and get back to the office."

"Oh. Well, you can at least tell me how the lesson went. You didn't get sick, did you?"

"No. No, I didn't." Julia couldn't resist smiling at that, but she quickly covered it with a scowl. "However, *Father,* don't think that lets you out of the doghouse. I'm still furious with you for getting me into this mess—not to mention concerned." Softening her expression she touched his arm. "Dad, don't you think we should make an appointment for you to see Dr. Wilbourne? Your recent behavior just hasn't been normal, even for you."

"A fine thing," Woody grumbled as he began plucking out the pink candles. "A man tries to help his daughter get over her fear of flying, and next thing he knows he's being accused of going senile."

Well used to his method of seeking sympathy to get out of being scolded, Julia pursed her lips and eyed him thoughtfully. "If you were so concerned, you could have given me a ticket to Hawaii as a present. The flight over might have terrified me, but at least I'd have enjoyed myself once I got there."

"What's Hawaii got that we don't? We live on Copano Bay. The entire Gulf of Mexico is practically in your backyard. How much more water do you need? Never mind," he added, barely pausing to take a breath. He peered at her over the dark rims of his glasses. "What else happened? You went to the airport to make an appointment for your first lesson and to your surprise Ethan could fit you in?"

"I went to ask for a refund. He said no." Julia's temper heated as she remembered what had accompanied the refusal. "The man was a complete boor about the whole thing. Not only did he refuse, he insulted and ridiculed me. In the end I had no choice but to call his bluff and take the first lesson." A slow smile of satisfaction replaced her frown. "I showed him, though, and I could tell he was surprised at how well I did."

"Then you're going to continue?" Woody asked, pausing in his task to watch her reaction.

Julia lifted her hands in a gesture of helplessness. "What choice do I have? You know perfectly well that I can barely stand missing out on double coupon day at the grocery store. Can you see me letting that instruction money go to waste?"

Woody carried the cake to the refrigerator to hide his satisfied smile. "I suppose not. But I want you to know I really appreciate you being so understanding about all this, Julia."

She shook her head, refusing to be such a soft touch. "Just promise you won't do anything impulsive again without checking with me first?" When her father nodded, she sighed, gave him a light kiss on his cheek and picked up her things from the table. "The cake is lovely. But I do have to get cleaned up and get back to city hall. Will I see you at the regular time for dinner?"

"Sure. But I don't want you to cook on your special day. Why don't we eat in town?"

"We eat too many meals out, as it is. I'll just pick up a couple of steaks for us on the way home."

Her father readily agreed, and Julia hurried off to her bedroom. Woody waited, listening until he could hear the door close behind her. Then he broke into a hushed whoop and slapped his thigh with pleasure.

"Hot damn!" he whispered excitedly. "Wait until Harlan hears this."

It took Julia two days, but she eventually settled back to a regular schedule at work. Wednesday found her finished with her chicken salad sandwich and at the collections window, covering for Bobbie Lee, who'd just left for her own lunch. Soon afterward a customer came in to pay her water bill, and Julia was standing there, stamping the woman's receipt, when Vernon Culpepper swaggered in.

She liked Vern well enough when they were talking one-on-one. Normally he was a responsible, thoughtful man, but she had a hard time remaining silent about that swagger. As the owner of Culpepper TV and Appliances, and the only Gator Cove businessman advertising on the local television station, Vern was the town's closest thing to a celebrity. The problem was he had a tendency to believe it himself.

"Thank you, Mrs. Smith. Have a good day," Julia said, giving the departing woman a warm smile before switching her gaze to Vern. He was wearing the outfit he'd worn in his Saint Patrick's Day Sale commercial—a green plaid sport coat, a tie that reminded her of leeks, and pants and a shirt in matching reseda. Julia concluded that the outfit might look festive on a leprechaun, but all it did for Vern was make him resemble a variegated bush. "Hello, Vern. I thought you always had your secretary bring in your water payments?"

"Didn't come to make a water payment, pretty lady," he drawled, smoothing back his lightly permed, salt-and-pepper hair and giving her the same, intimate wink he used at the end of each commercial. "Came to make you a proposition you couldn't refuse."

He must have come from lunching with one of his suppliers, Julia thought, her spirits deflating like a punctured balloon. He knew she didn't care for sales pitches, and normally he conscientiously avoided using that smooth-talking approach on her, but apparently this was one of those occasions when he forgot himself.

"This isn't the best time for me to talk," Julia replied, dutifully depositing Mrs. Smith's check and statement in the proper tray. "There are strict rules about personal business infringing on work time here." That wasn't exactly true, but she was intent on maintaining her professional decorum.

"Aw, Julia. You can make an exception for me, can't you? This is something that can't wait."

"Really? Well, I suppose in that case it would be all right." But she was still aware of the curious and amused looks of the remaining people in the building—Lucille at the computer and Inez, who was

Mayor Bainbridge's secretary. Even Ted Harcourt, the city manager, was leaning over so he could watch through the open door of his office. She knew why they were so curious. Men simply didn't call on the ever business-minded and efficient Julia Woods. In fact, except for an occasional visit from her father—when he locked himself out of the house or his truck and needed to borrow her spare keys— no one ever came to call on her at work.

More self-conscious than flattered, Julia lifted a hand to her bun. "What is it that you needed to talk about?"

"Well, as you know, the Southwest Furniture and Appliance Show is in Houston this week. Mother was going to go with me, but she's not completely recovered from that bunion operation yet. How about taking her place? We'd leave early Saturday morning and make a day of it. There's even a restaurant near the convention center that's offering two-for-one dinners for anyone with a show pass."

Julia wanted to crawl under the counter when she heard Inez titter. It was one thing to attend an occasional movie with Vern or to sit on her front porch and discuss the latest best-seller, but she *didn't* have serious feelings for him, and—what with him devoting himself to the care of his mother—he certainly didn't have any for her. The last thing she needed was for people to get the wrong idea about them.

"I— I'm not sure, Vern."

"It was Mother's idea."

Because his mother considered her harmless and no threat, Julia thought with a fleeting, ironic smile. Wouldn't it be nice if, just once, she wasn't so easy to classify and dismiss? Wouldn't it be fun to be considered—well, a little mysterious, even sexy? She glanced down at her ringless hands. Of course, the municipality would probably have a collective stroke if she ever tried anything that was remotely shocking. People raised their eyebrows when she so much as indulged in adding a bit of color to her clear nail polish.

"Excuse me for interrupting your cozy conversation, but does a taxpayer have to wait all day to be taken care of around here?"

At the sound of Ethan's sarcastic voice, Julia glanced up to find him towering over Vern's shoulder. As always, his flame-tipped hair was in rebellion against any law of order, and his black T-shirt stretched from shoulder to shoulder, as if the man were still a boy outgrowing his clothes. But it was his scowl she noticed most; the way it made his windburned features appear craggy and tough, it canceled any further thoughts of boys. As her eyes locked with his, Julia felt her heartbeat skid to a stop

like a kitten trying to do the same on a newly pol-
ished linoleum floor. Ethan never had to worry about
his sex appeal. Even now, despite his mood, it oozed
from his whiskey-brown eyes with a hundred-
twenty-proof punch.

Julia moistened her dry lips. He must have over-
heard Vern's invitation and been annoyed when she
didn't immediately reply that she had a previous
commitment for the day. But she was hesitant about
making that announcement; so far only Bobbie Lee
knew about the flying lessons, and Julia wanted to
keep it that way as long as possible. She decided it
would be prudent to take care of Ethan first and get
him out of the building.

"Pardon me for a moment, Vern. Ethan must be
in a hurry. What can I do for you?" she asked the
taller man with formal politeness.

"I have something that needs to be notarized."
He handed her a folded sheet of paper.

Julia was one of only two notaries in the community, and the only one who didn't charge for her
services; thus, most of Gator Cove's notary work
came to her. She quickly perused the affidavit and
nodded. "All right. It'll only take me a moment."
To keep him from conversing with Vern, she slid a
notebook toward him. "Perhaps you'd like to read
this while you're waiting. It's a petition proposing

a change in our town's name I'm going to present to the city council.''

"What for?''

"Because Gator Cove is hardly a respectable name for a dignified community such as ours.''

"It suits me well enough.''

Julia's answering look told him she wasn't surprised. "Consider it from someone else's viewpoint, a parent's, for example. Their children grow up and go off to college or enter the work force.... Would you find it easy to admit you came from a town named *Gator Cove?*''

"Sure.''

She should have known better than to put it that way. Julia decided to try another approach. "All right, but what about being factual? We all know that before the town lake was purchased, it supposedly was inhabited by a stray alligator or two, and that the owner became known as Gator Bill because he'd allegedly wrestled a calf from one. But except for the papier-mâché alligator some high-school seniors tossed into the lake a few years ago, there's never been a substantiated sighting.''

"There've been some.''

"Really? Then where's the evidence?''

"How should I know? Anyway, who's going to argue with something that's eight feet long and has razor-sharp teeth? If it decided it didn't want to hang around to have its picture taken, I know *I* wouldn't challenge it to a wrestling match.''

A sound, suspiciously similar to a guffaw, came from Ted Harcourt's office. Even as Julia wished magic hands would jerk the city manager's chair out from beneath him, she wasn't surprised at his reaction. Men. Why was it that whenever they disagreed with a woman, they had a juvenile habit of trying to make her appear foolish? Even Vern was grinning—so hard she could see most of his gums. She was tempted to remind him that his signature was the second one on the petition, following his mother's.

"Oh, never mind," she snapped with a toss of her head. Having had more than her fill of the lot of them, she pivoted neatly on her heel and strode to her desk, where she kept her logbook and notary seal. She'd half completed the entry when she heard Ethan howl with laughter.

"Serenity?" he croaked, having read the rest of the petition. "You want to change the name to *Serenity Cove*? You call that an improvement?"

"It's a lovely name," Julia replied with a frozen smile.

"It's a wimpy name. And I'll tell you something else. There may or may not be any alligators around here, but there sure as heck isn't a whole lot of serenity, either."

Julia was so indignant, so furious, she was surprised her grip on her notary seal didn't punch a hole straight through Ethan's affidavit. "Look who's complaining," she replied with artificial sweetness as she returned to the counter and thrust the paper at him. "The man who's been served more citations for disturbing the peace than any other resident in the community."

Ethan felt his eyes burn with anger. He told himself he should have known better than to come in here and waste his time on this exasperating icon to preserved virginity. Why he'd been feeling generous and had even been tempted to offer to lend her a book on flying was beyond him. He would have to plead temporary insanity for even considering the gesture.

"Don't forget our appointment for Saturday. There's a penalty charge for not showing up for a lesson," he said, crushing the affidavit in his fist.

"Lesson—what lesson?" Vern asked, his wide-eyed gaze bouncing from Ethan to Julia.

She ignored the question. "Maybe I'd like to reschedule."

Ethan couldn't believe his ears. Was she actually daring to add insult to injury by telling him that she would rather spend the day with this, this *peacock* gawking beside him? "No rescheduling—" he enunciated with a patience he hardly felt. "Unless it's due to inclement weather or mechanical problems with the plane."

"Then I guess the odds are in my favor, since we already know what great shape it's in," she muttered ungraciously.

A spider mite on the nearby philodendron plant could have sneezed, and it would have been heard in the silence following Ethan's abrupt departure. Julia was aware of every eye in the place being on her, but she focused on Vern. He looked more confused than upset, and that was the only reassuring thing about explaining the situation to him.

"So you see, I'm not going to be able to go to Houston with you, Vern," she concluded a short time later, still trying to keep her voice low. "I'd truly forgotten all about the appointment."

"I can't believe it," he replied, far louder than Julia would have liked.

"Shh...listen, Vern, could we keep this—?"

"Flying lessons! What do you suppose got into your father?"

About a pint of sour-mash whiskey and maybe a few beer chasers, Julia thought, her heart sinking as Lucille gasped and Inez tittered again. So much for her secret. Of course, she'd known it was just a matter of time before it got out, anyway, what with Kenny Spivet working at the airport office and attending the same church she did. By the end of next

Sunday's service, the news would be all over the congregation. Still, she would have liked a few more days to get used to the idea herself before becoming the focus of local gossip. Darn Ethan for his big, spiteful mouth.

Damn that woman for her waspish tongue. As Ethan drove across town toward Rocky's Bar and Grill, he gripped the old Jeep's steering wheel and fantasized it was Julia's throat. It would have served her right if he'd made it easy for her to go to Houston with Culpepper.

Why didn't you?

Because she'd already made the appointment with him, and he didn't like having his schedules upset.

Since when? Procrastination may not be your middle name, but seasons have been known to change before you notice someone hasn't shown up for an appointment. Admit it, your ego was bruised.

He bristled and swore under his breath. His ego bruised? Ha. That would be the day. It was Julia, that was all. She'd been a pain in the neck when they were kids, and by now she'd honed the talent into a surgical art form. If she wanted Culpepper, that was no skin off his nose. They deserved each other.

Minutes later he turned into Rocky's gravel-covered parking lot. The bar and grill was a weatherworn building on stilts that partially extended into Texas's Copano Bay. Owned by a statuesque Scandinavian widow who'd shortened her name from Gretchen Van Rosenbeck to Rocky, it had become a home away from home for an assortment of characters such as his father and Woody, people who needed a place to get out of the sun, yet weren't interested in a home life or gainful employment. Ethan liked the place because Rocky served the best plate lunches around for the cheapest price.

When he walked inside, it was barely one in the afternoon. The regular lunch crowd was lingering for a second beer, and the all-dayers were already back to their games of poker, checkers or watching envious flies collect on the outside of Rocky's screened windows.

After halfheartedly waving to a few people who shouted greetings, Ethan went to the far table by the windows that looked out over the bay. It was Harlan's and Woody's table, and now he slumped into the chair beside his father.

"Hey," Harlan said, glancing up from the cards he was dealing. "You look like you swallowed a raw egg."

"My appetite's almost ruined, as it is," Ethan replied sourly. "Don't finish the job, okay?"

"Uh-oh. What's the matter now?"

"I just came from city hall. You can guess the rest."

"Julia." Woody sighed as he spoke.

"Have a beer," Harlan said, signaling Rocky, "and tell us all about it."

Ethan shook his head. "No beer. Somebody's coming to look at the crop duster this afternoon, and they'll want a test flight."

"Hi, gorgeous," Rocky said, arriving at the table and giving him a friendly pat on the back.

Turning slightly, Ethan shot the buxom, platinum blonde a crooked smile. "Hiya, Rocky. How about sending over today's special and the biggest glass of ice tea you have?"

"You look like you could use something stronger than ice tea, kiddo."

"Yeah, well, the spirit might be willing, but the FAA has this thing about pilots flying under the influence. Thanks for the concern, though."

When the middle-aged woman withdrew, Harlan shot Woody a speaking glance before leaning elbow to elbow with his son. "What's the problem?"

"The problem is that oil and vinegar don't mix," Ethan replied, slowly turning the saltshaker in the middle of the table. "Neither do cats and dogs...and right now I wouldn't put too much money on chickens and roosters."

"He and Julia had an argument," Woody explained to Harlan.

"I *know* that much," his friend replied testily. He turned back to his son. "What about?"

"She wants to rename this place Serenity Cove. Can you believe it? Besides that, she had an appointment with me for Saturday, and she's about to go to Houston with Vern Culpepper."

"His commercials are stupid," Woody replied glumly.

Harlan shot his friend an impatient look before turning back to his son. "What do you mean, 'about to'? Is she going, or is she taking her lesson?"

"How the hell should I know? I was so angry I left," Ethan said, pushing back from the table. "Excuse me. I've got to go wash up."

As soon as he was out of earshot, Harlan leaned over the table toward Woody. "You and your bright ideas. I told you this wouldn't work!"

"Oh, sure you did. Right at first, maybe, but after you thought about all those fringe benefits with having a daughter-in-law, you were practically rabid over the idea," Woody replied, pushing up his glasses and matching him glare for glare. After a moment, however, he shrugged. "It's early yet. Give them time."

"Time for what? To kill each other? At least

you've got another kid out there somewhere. Ethan's all I've got left in the world.''

Woody picked up the cards Harlan had just dealt him and patiently rearranged them. ''Haven't you ever heard of that old saying about there being a fine line between hate and love? As hot under the collar as Ethan seems, I think we may be on to something big, Harl.''

''Yeah,'' Harlan muttered, reaching for his beer mug. ''Our joint funerals, if either of them ever wise up to what we've done. How many cards you want?''

''I guess I could keep these.''

Harlan dragged a hand over his face. ''You and your damned straights. And Ethan thinks he's having a lousy day.''

Chapter Four

When Saturday arrived, Ethan had a hard time convincing himself he should get out of bed, let alone show up at the airport. For a few minutes he considered drifting off to sleep again; he wasn't in the mood for another verbal skirmish with Julia, that is, if she even came.

But he finally did rise, and after a brisk shower and a second cup of strong, black coffee, he reminded himself that he had plenty of work waiting for him, whether she arrived for her lesson or not. What was more, work would help keep his mind off her. Buoyed by the thought that his day might not have to start out with squabbling, after all, he snatched up the last, stale doughnut from the card-

board box on the otherwise empty shelf in the refrigerator and headed out to his Jeep.

His first real glimpse of what kind of weather the
day offered added to his brightening mood. The flat,
coastal terrain provided a panoramic view of the
sky, which was a violet blue this morning. There
were only a few, wispy cirrus clouds to compete
with its drama, and though he always paid close attention to cloud formations, he dismissed these,
since they were already dissipating and were at a far
higher altitude than the five thousand feet or under
he usually flew the trainer. The breeze was minimal
and directly from the south. It was a perfect day for
flying.

Maybe after he completed the task of inventory-
ing all those parts for the financial statement the
bank wanted, he could take up the stunt plane. He
would have liked to go flying first, anything to avoid
doing all that paperwork. But getting those account-
ing figures had to take precedence, if he wanted serious consideration for that loan he was going to
apply for.

Preoccupied with those thoughts, he quickly covered the short distance to the airport. It was odd,
though; he rarely daydreamed, and as a result, it left
him feeling slightly out of sync and disorientated—
so much so that he almost drove past his own han-

gar. Spotting Julia there, waiting for him, quickly snapped him out of that.

Or was that Julia?

The car was hers, he thought, parking beside it, but there was something strikingly different about the woman. Gone was the prim Victorian who disapprovingly peered at him through tortoiseshell glasses like a younger version of his grade-school librarian. Yes, the glasses were the same, and maybe she was still eyeing him with disapproval, but as for the rest...

She looked like a sprig of heather plucked from a mountainside, her blouse and slacks a combination of mauve and raspberry that the sunlight seemed particularly intent on emphasizing. Because she'd always hidden herself beneath clothes that either obliterated her shape entirely or rigidly confined it in boxlike angles—as did those masculinely tailored suits she seemed particularly fond of—he was stunned to discover the feminine curves they'd been concealing. With wonder he noted a ballerina's small breasts, surprisingly long legs, the waist and hips of a nymph.

What mush. Ethan gave himself a mental shake, wondering if next he would be quoting poetry!

He rubbed at his eyes and looked again. No, this wasn't an optical illusion. She was real.

He noticed that her hair was different, too. That

hideous knot into which she tortured her hair had been abandoned for something that was, though no less neat, far more youthful and soft. The French braid also flattered her fine features. Not sure it was his wisest move, he killed the engine and climbed out of the Jeep.

Julia had expected some surprise—truth be known, she'd *hoped* for some—but reality being what it was, she found that Ethan's intense scrutiny gave her goose bumps. They weren't the kind she used to get from watching scary movies. Actually they felt rather wicked and wonderful, but nevertheless made her shiver.

"You—uh—look different," he told her.

Self-conscious, she glanced down at herself. "I thought if I was expected to crawl all over and under an airplane, I'd better wear something that wouldn't get in the way."

"A pair of old jeans and a T-shirt would have sufficed."

It described exactly what he was wearing, except that today the T-shirt was white and looked fairly new. If Julia was a gambler, she would have bet his entire wardrobe consisted of jeans and T-shirts. She, on the other hand, hadn't even owned anything denim in high school, and except for a few pairs of faded culottes, which she wore when working in the yard, her clothes closet contained nothing but office attire. A trip to the local dress shop had been necessary to come up with this outfit. She thought it was an improvement and didn't hesitate to tell him so.

Oh, yes, it was an improvement, Ethan thought darkly. That was the problem; he didn't want to notice how much of an improvement it was or, more particularly, how affected he was by it.

"It's fine," he muttered, feigning an indifferent shrug. "But I thought you'd made other plans for today?"

"You told me no rescheduling."

"Since when did you pay attention to anything I said?"

"I knew it," she said to the world in general. "If I didn't show up, you would have been furious. I'm here and you're still grumbling. What's it take to please you?"

"A woman who doesn't talk so much." He turned away to unlock the hangar doors. "I've got a lot to do today, so if you're here to work, fine. Let's get to it."

Julia didn't consider herself inordinately thin-skinned, but his curt reply hurt as much as it annoyed her. She wasn't expecting miracles, but did he have to be such a wretch? Would it have mortally injured the man to say she looked nice? Did he think that she was so hard up that she would construe a kind word as a proposal of marriage?

"I've got a lot to do today," she mimicked silently, glaring at his back through narrowed eyes as he rolled open the doors. Well, he could grouse like a bad-tempered boar all he wanted. She was determined that for once he wasn't going to get the best of her temper. Tucking her keys into her pants pocket and slapping her logbook against her thigh, she followed him.

Two returned phone calls and a terrible cup of instant coffee later, Ethan led her back outside to do the preflight inspection of the Cessna. Julia's determination to approach this with a positive attitude waned somewhat when she found herself doubting how much she remembered from the first lesson. Certain she was going to need a complete review, she was surprised and delighted to discover she got through most of the checklist on her own. As a result, when she did forget something or made a mistake, Ethan's abrupt or sarcastic correction was harder to take. By the time she rounded the front of the plane to climb into the cockpit, her nerves were as frayed as the bottoms of his jeans.

"Hey!" he barked, pointing to the wooden chocks bracketing the wheels. "Are you going to move these, or are we supposed to try to roll over them?"

Retracing her steps, Julia grabbed the braided nylon rope and jerked the barriers free. But before she went to do the same to the other wheel, she turned to face Ethan. "May I say something?"

He eyed her hands-on-hips stance a moment before replying. "Is anybody stopping you?"

"Yes, you. You've been in a bad mood ever since you arrived, though considering you're the one who was late, I had more of a right to be annoyed than you did. Now I don't know what your problem is, but I'm trying to be professional about this. Two mature people should be able to get through an hour of instruction together without biting each other's heads off."

Ready to shoot back another caustic reply, Ethan caught himself. She was right. He had been acting like one of the antagonists in a Dr. Seuss book, which might have been forgivable, even amusing, when they were young. But they weren't kids anymore.

He dropped his gaze to her pink and white jogging shoes, which also had that squeaky-clean, new look. They were about half the size of his, another poignant reminder of how unfair and bullyish he was being. He rubbed the back of his neck. "Hell."

Julia gave a ladylike sniff. "You call that an apology?"

"Give me a minute, all right?" When she lifted

an eyebrow in skepticism, he crossed his arms over his chest. "All right, I'm sorry. I don't know... maybe I'm more worried about the business and things than I thought. Anyway," he concluded gruffly, "I apologize for acting like a jerk."

It surprised Julia how ready she was to forgive him and how generous she felt as a result. She extended her hand. "Peace?"

"You and me? That would be one for the record books," he drawled, giving her a crooked smile. But even as she chuckled, he closed his hand around hers. "Peace."

Julia's agitated pulse rate barely had time to calm before she felt it accelerate again. Intimacy. She'd always wondered about that indescribable closeness that came when certain people clicked. Chemistry. Secretly she craved it, but had never dreamed that the first hint of such a feeling would come with Ethan. Yet as their gazes held, whatever it was that was arcing between them intensified, heated. It made her feel feminine and desirable, even as she gave in to panic and withdrew her hand.

"I should apologize, too, since I'm partly to blame myself," she said softly, hoping he wasn't thinking she was throwing herself at him. She knew she wasn't his type. "I haven't exactly been a good sport about this whole flying thing...and if I'd paid more attention during my last lesson, I wouldn't be making these kinds of mistakes. I can appreciate that it's annoying to you."

"It's part of being a beginner."

"You're just saying that to be nice."

"No, it's true. Who knows, maybe Lindbergh or Earhart were naturals, but as for the rest of us, we all suffered through our difficult moments."

Julia smiled. "I don't believe you ever had trouble remembering chocks."

For several seconds Ethan simply stared at her, wondering if she had any idea how her face lit up when she smiled. "Chocks? No...but I once took up a plane that had only one fuel tank filled, thinking that it was more than enough to get me where I was going, and I ended up landing two miles short of the runway, on some rancher's driveway. Luckily he wasn't one of those people who liked to plant trees along it, otherwise I would have had to land in the pasture and try to outrun his prize longhorn bull."

"From now on that's the *first* thing I'm going to check," Julia said, shivering at the thought of finding herself in such a predicament. "I know I would never be able to stay coolheaded and look for an alternate landing site in a situation like that."

They were standing only a few feet apart, and her response, coupled with his own understanding of how easily it could happen to her, touched Ethan acutely and left him with the strongest urge to reach out to her somehow. Bemused, he glanced away. "Your father—er, Woody, mentioned something about your fear of flying. Is it something you can talk about?"

"You'll probably think it's silly."

"Fear is never silly, and believe me, I've heard all sorts of stories. Try me," he murmured, his voice husky with encouragement.

She fingered the braid resting on her shoulder, struggling with the decision whether to risk sharing that much of herself or not. No matter how nice it was that they were actually speaking civilly, their history made wariness instinctive. Yet she was the one who'd made the appeal for better relations. How could she expect him to try, if she wasn't willing to?

"When I was seven, my mother and I flew to Arkansas for my grandmother's funeral," she began, focusing on the checklist she held. "It was late spring, and the plane was the small, commuter type. We got caught in a storm, and I remember at one point even the flight attendants appeared anxious. Anyway, my mother was already upset over her mother's death, so by the time we landed she was a wreck. She refused to even consider flying back, and we took a bus."

"I think I remember Woody and my father talking about that," Ethan said, nodding slowly. He shot her a sympathetic look. "Not long afterward your mother became ill herself and died."

It seemed a lifetime ago, Julia thought with a sad sigh. Sometimes she could barely remember what her mother had looked like. "Logically I know one incident has nothing to do with the other. But to this day I still associate flying with death."

"You were a kid."

"Were. I'm a grown woman now."

Somewhere inside Ethan heard a whispered *amen* to that. He cleared his throat. "I'm no expert, but I would say that recognizing the problem is half the battle," he said, offering her a reassuring smile. "And look—you've already cleared a few hurdles by taking your first lesson. Cut yourself some slack."

His words and the hesitant, almost shy warmth in his eyes sparked flashes of pleasure in Julia. She quickly lowered her own gaze. What *was* this? Julia Woods feeling anything but frustration or irritation for Ethan Ross? Impossible, unless someone had accidentally put something into the local water supply. "You know what?" she asked, fidgeting with the notebook she held. "You're absolutely right. And today I'm going to jump another hurdle. Let's go!"

"Are you feeling okay?"

They'd just completed their takeoff and were leveling out at a thousand feet. Julia nodded to Ethan and risked taking one hand off the steering wheel long enough to wipe her damp palm against her slacks. "This time I could hear almost everything you and Kenny said on the radio, and I think I'm beginning to understand the jargon. But I still have my doubts about ever being able to actually fly this by myself."

"That's a defeatist attitude. Say it enough and you'll convince yourself."

"There is such a thing as reality and knowing your limitations."

"We're going to practice turns today!" Ethan shouted above the engine's roar.

"Ignoring me isn't going to make me do any better. I didn't say I wouldn't *try*. I just said I didn't believe the day would come when you'd trust me to be alone in this thing."

"You're looking too far into the future," he replied, while scanning the skies for other aircraft that might be in the area. "Worry about getting through today. Now—remembering what I told you about turns, I want you to ease into a right one," he said mildly. She turned the wheel, the Cessna banked, but barely changed course. "Not that easily. We don't carry enough fuel to circle the entire state."

"Very funny," she replied, though she was secretly pleased that he hadn't growled this time. "I'm turning the wheel to the right, and it's dipping the wing, but that's all."

"Remember what I told you last time about co-ordinated turns? Use the rudders in conjunction with the wheel. The right rudder in this case, which will sling the plane's tail to the left. Wait!" Just as she began to execute the maneuver, Ethan moderated the position of the wheel. "Call me a fossil, but I prefer my students to master simple flying before getting into daredevil stunts, unless you warn me to bring a parachute along."

"I thought you told me that a parachute would probably be worthless at the altitude we generally fly?"

"That's right, but I also told you we were doing turns, not loops, so *don't* pull out the wheel as you turn, okay?"

Though his tone was dry, the rebuke didn't hold the sarcastic sting Julia had grown accustomed to through the years. Risking a glance his way, she found that his expression lacked censure. Relieved that he really did seem to be striving for patience with her, she did her best to complete the turn.

"Do another," Ethan said, without rating her performance.

"Did I do something wrong?"

"No, but do another anyway."

He could at least have said she did all right, she

fumed, compressing her lips and taking a deep breath to settle her stomach. After all, banking to where the passenger's window gave them a bird's-eye view of the lush, green fields on the north side of town wasn't her idea of fun.

As much as she found right turns unsettling, left turns were absolutely terrifying. She tried to avert her face so that she wouldn't have to look at the ground that from this angle looked much closer than fifteen hundred feet below. "Do these doors ever open, say, accidentally?"

"I've never heard of it happening. But no sweat if it did, you still have your seat belt," Ethan replied nonchalantly. "Try another of those and make it tighter. Get that wing down."

Julia gave her seat belt an extra tug to tighten the straps across her chest and waist until she felt the pressure clear to her back. Hollywood might have its sidewalk of the stars, but she was determined that these vinyl seats would eternally carry the imprint of her bottom. What a world, she thought, trying to make sense of the irony wherein humans could solve the mystery of flight, while the dodo bird—who could really have used a break—never got more than a few inches off the ground. Mentally shaking her head, she gripped the wheel with perspiration-slick hands and began the turn.

Thirty minutes later Julia placed a hand to her stomach, knowing she'd reached her limit. She shot Ethan an entreating look.

"What's the matter? Jumped enough hurdles for one day?"

"I've got news for you," she replied dryly. "I feel like I tackled the Great Wall of China. Literally."

Ethan had to glance out his own window to hide his amusement. "Do one more to the left—that's still your weak side—and we'll take her in."

But Julia knew that would be one too many and shook her head. "I don't know what you had for breakfast, Ethan, or how you manage to keep it down. However, if these feet don't walk on something solid soon, I'm fairly certain I'll end up showing you what mine consisted of. What do you say I give you an IOU and we call it a day?"

Seeing that her face did indeed appear pinched and wore a greenish cast, Ethan gave her instructions to do a right-handed approach to the airport. "Take a deep breath—watch your air speed.... Your Stall buzzer's going to go off.... Keep your nose up."

The instructions came with a machine gun's endless volley until perspiration seemed to be pouring down every inch of Julia's body. She had to look a mess. She *knew* she was exhausted. But when she heard the plane's tires chirp on the runway and felt the reassuring solidity of earth beneath her, everything paled beside the glowing sense of achievement that was even stronger than after her last time up.

Following Ethan's directions, she taxied the plane to the hangar and shut down the engine. "That was okay," she murmured to herself, breaking into a whimsical smile when she realized she really meant it.

The sun had risen considerably and was approaching its midpoint in the sky, but as she glanced out through the windshield, everything else looked the same. In the distance she could see people walking into the main office. Several at other hangars were working on their own planes.... Everyone was oblivious of her achievement. It was incredible. Shouldn't someone have noticed? Shouldn't something have changed? *She* felt different.

"Make sure everything's off and secured," Ethan told her, unfastening his seat belt. "And don't forget to log your time."

As he climbed out of the plane, Julia stared in disbelief. "Wait a minute!" Hastily shutting down and releasing her own belt, she dragged herself out of her side. "Ethan—hey!"

He turned to see her sprinting toward him. Something twitched deep in his chest as he noticed the ordeal had wilted his sprig of heather—but, he mused wryly, she still had a feisty glint in her eye.

"Didn't you forget something?" she demanded breathlessly.

Once again he eyed those hands she placed on her hips. "I don't think so. Oh, right—your next lesson. When do you want it? I can squeeze you in most any weekday, preferably after three or before noon on Saturdays."

"No, not my next lesson. This one," she replied impatiently, brushing at the wisps of hair that stuck to her cheek and wiping at the moisture trickling down her throat. "Aren't you going to critique my performance, tell me if I did a good job or not?"

He watched her push her glasses up her nose, only to have them slide back down. "If this wasn't so stubby," he drawled, pushing up the glasses for her and then tweaking her nose, "maybe you wouldn't have that problem."

"You're a real comedian, Ethan."

Tilting his head, his expression turned speculative. "Ever consider wearing contacts, so you wouldn't have to put up with glasses at all?"

Immediately she began to withdraw. "Great. Next we're going to hear your repertoire of 'four-eyes' jokes."

"Whoa," he said, grasping her arm before she could turn away. "I was talking about comfort, not looks. Hell, look at me. I'm the last person to make fun of someone else's appearance.''

Was he crazy? He might not be Fifth Avenue, New York-model-perfect, but he was the epitome of Texas-rugged. That appealed to women. Otherwise he wouldn't have so many of the ladies in town casting him inviting looks. And sure, Julia thought, nibbling at her lower lip, she'd thought about contact lenses, especially during those high-school years when her classmates would be asked out on dates and she stayed home. But she'd always assumed that contacts cost much more than glasses. Her father's military pension had supported them satisfactorily, but it didn't allow for too many extravagances. Nowadays she was so used to the glasses, she just hadn't thought about trying anything else.

''Ethan,'' she said, hoping to regain the rapport they'd experienced earlier. ''Stop fishing for compliments and changing the subject. Did I or didn't I do okay up there today?''

''You did okay.''

Julia glanced heavenward. ''Hallelujah—a kind word!'' When she lowered her gaze, her eyes were twinkling. ''Now was that so difficult?''

''Maybe not quite as bad as a trip to the dentist. Since when did *you* start fishing for compliments, Mouse?''

"I'm human. Everyone likes to have their ego stroked once in a while. Even you, I'll bet."

Ethan lifted his left eyebrow at the openly teasing remark and broke into an irreverent grin. "Why, yes, ma'am. Stroke my ego, and I roll over and purr louder than that big tomcat of ours. Want to try it sometime and see?"

A strange excitement gave Julia the courage to grin back at him. "Oh, Ethan, Ethan. You have playing hard-to-get down to a real science."

He chuckled and tossed his head. "Go on, scram, Mouse. I told you I have work to do."

"Will next Saturday be okay? Same time?"

"Sure," he replied, surprised when his first re-action was that next Saturday seemed a helluva long way off. As he watched her head for her car, he was also surprised to note that she had an attractive bounce in her step that hadn't been there before. Actually, what was attractive was the trim shape of her bottom. His expression grew whimsical.

Someone cleared his throat, and startled, Ethan turned to find his father standing beside him. "Where did you come from?" he asked, not at all pleased to find himself at a disadvantage.

Harlan ignored the question and watched Julia drive away. "That was a real interesting exchange just now. I thought you said you two weren't getting along?"

"We decided to be mature and professional about things," Ethan replied, turning toward his Jeep and pretending a great interest in a scratch that was so old, it was rusting.

"Uh-huh."

Glancing over his shoulder, Ethan saw that his father wasn't buying any of it. He exhaled in frustration. "Wipe that foolish grin off your face, and let's go inside and get a beer."

"You just told Julia you were busy."

"Never mind what I told her," Ethan muttered, turning away and kicking at a clump of earth. "I'm dryer than this dirt. You want one or not?"

"How can I turn down such a gracious invitation?" Harlan replied, all innocence. But as Ethan walked into the hangar, the older man rubbed his hands together. "Maybe things aren't as hopeless as I thought," he murmured to himself. Then he called to his son, "But only one, my boy! I promised Woody I'd meet him for lunch."

Chapter Five

Spring was Julia's favorite season, but as May slipped into June she realized that she was barely aware of this one's passing. Everything seemed to be moving so fast. No sooner did she get to work on Monday than it was Saturday and time for another flying lesson. What was most surprising was discovering that the hour couldn't come soon enough. Why? Because the impossible had happened—she'd caught the bug.

Somewhere during her second or third lesson flying became fun. Gone was the feeling that her father had painted a dark cloud over her head, threatening her otherwise peaceful existence. Occasionally she even took two lessons a week. Learning to be a good pilot became a challenge to master; each hour she took up the Cessna was now an adventure to experience to the fullest; each accomplishment filled her with an almost giddy sense of achievement. And she knew she owed it all to Ethan.

Ever since her second session, when she'd challenged him to treat her with the respect due an adult, things had changed between them. Granted, he still teased her when she forgot the proper name for a gauge or overcompensated in a turn, but it was a gentler teasing, always followed by words of approval when she corrected the error. He'd also lent her a few books to help her get a better perception of flying and never seemed to mind answering her many questions. Actually she was beginning to believe he even looked forward to them.

Their relationship had become decidedly friendly, and, though the conservative in her carefully pointed out the difference between that and true friendship, she was grateful for it. After years of being at odds with each other, almost anything was an improvement. Once or twice, when she found him watching her in an odd, almost perplexed way, she wondered what it would be like if something more developed. But common sense kept those thoughts in check. She had seen the type of woman Ethan went out with; he liked them colorful, curvaceous, and as casual as he was in their approach to relationships. She didn't have to look into a mirror to know that she bore no resemblance to any of them, either physically or intellectually.

However, like any red-blooded female with a touch of spring fever, she did put her rejuvenated spirits to adventurous—though Bobbie Lee smugly called it predictable—use. She made an appointment with an optometrist and had herself fitted for contact lenses. The transformation had everyone saying she resembled a young Audrey Hepburn, and slightly dazed by all the compliments, she even let Bobbie Lee talk her into a trip to the drugstore, where they added more items to her sparse inventory of cosmetics. Bobbie Lee swore a little eyeliner here and a touch of blush there would have men drooling over her. It left Julia with the nagging impulse to invest in a can of disinfectant spray, just in case.

When she experimented with the cosmetics in the privacy of her own bathroom, she ended up dispensing with most of them, deciding she'd settle for an occasional admiring glance. And by the second Saturday in June, as she drove to the airport, she still had yet to admit *who* she hoped the admirer would be.

Her heart was pounding harder than on the day she'd driven her first new car off the lot at Oscar Mooney's dealership. Adjusting the rearview mirror to check her appearance, she almost ran the four-

way Stop sign near the airport entrance. It was a
good thing she'd decided not to use the blush; her
cheeks were already a feverish pink, despite having
the air conditioner on full force. Should she have
skipped the eyeliner, as well? It did emphasize her
eyes, but perhaps it was too much for daytime. What
if she got something under her lenses and her eyes
began to tear? She hadn't checked to see if she'd
purchased waterproof items.

By the time she parked beside Ethan's Jeep, her
stomach was upset, and she was a second away from
shifting into Reverse and racing home to scrub her
face. But a quick glance at her watch told her she
had only five minutes to spare before her appointment. As improved as her relations were with Ethan,
he would have plenty to say if she was late, especially if she couldn't come up with a legitimate excuse. Deciding that in all probability he wouldn't
say more than two words about how different she
looked, she took a deep breath, shut off the engine
and climbed out of the car.

From inside the hangar she heard the sound of file
drawers slamming and a deep, familiar voice swear-
ing. Musing to herself about how other things *never*
changed, Julia went inside.

She found him in his office, squatting before the
bottom file drawer, impatiently tugging out one
folder after another while muttering under his

breath. Julia felt a wry smile curve her lips as she leaned against the doorjamb and crossed her arms. "You need a keeper, Ethan."

"Tell me about it," he replied without turning around. "It's getting so I can't find anything around here anymore."

"I wonder why."

"Don't get smart. You work in an office. What kind of filing system would straighten out this mess?"

"None, because you have a habitual disregard for putting things back where you found them."

About to protest, Ethan pivoted on the balls of his feet. He didn't give Julia an admiring look. What he gave her was a wide-eyed stare and then an eyebrow-raising oath, then he lost his balance and plopped onto the floor with a heavy thump.

Julia didn't know whether to laugh or hunt for a paper bag to drag over her head. Did this qualify in the category of knocking a man off his feet? "Well, say something," she entreated endless seconds later, when he failed to make any additional response.

"Uh-oh."

"What kind of reaction is that?"

The kind a man makes when he's had the rug pulled from out under him. The kind Dr. Frankenstein probably had after creating his monster. The kind of reaction Tarzan wished he'd had the guts to make, when Jane casually mentioned a cozy, thatched hut downriver that had three bedrooms and a two-elephant garage.

Giving himself a mental shake, he wiped at the beads of sweat that had formed on his forehead and upper lip. He really needed to do something about the air circulation in this place. "You, um, you're not wearing your glasses."

"I took your advice and got contacts. What do you think?"

She'd knocked him onto his backside, but obviously she didn't agree that a picture was worth a thousand words. Unfortunately, words weren't his strong suit. He thought she looked nice...all right, terrific. Softer. Touchable. Her outfit, a pair of turquoise slacks and a matching, striped top gave her a fresh, sporty appeal. With her hair falling in loose waves around her shoulders and tied back by a matching ribbon, she could pass for one of those college kids that came to the coast during spring and summer breaks. In comparison he felt grimy, not nearly as young, yet dangerously tempted to cross the room and taste those petal-pink lips. But he was damned if he was going to tell her any of that.

Why had he ever believed that this was one woman who would play fair?

Get a hold of yourself, he commanded, pushing

himself to his feet. *She's not playing at all. It's not her fault you didn't notice her potential before.*

"I'm—" Ethan laughed self-consciously "—speechless." And he was going to give his father an earful when he found him. The old buzzard had to have known about this. The least he could have done was prepare him. Julia was going to think he was a randy bull seeing his first heifer.

"The doctor said that it would take a while to adjust to these lenses," Julia told him, uncomfortable with the silence that kept spreading between them.

"You changed your hair, too."

"It was time for a trim."

"It's nice." He watched pleasure blossom on her face, as if he'd just told her she was the most beautiful woman on earth. The room went from uncomfortably small and hot to unbearably claustrophobic. "So—are you ready to get to work?"

"You bet!"

Despite everything, her enthusiasm amused him. It was refreshing to see that veil of propriety giving way and a different, less inhibited Julia emerge. With a silent chuckle over the incongruous pattern of his thoughts lately, he crossed the room and gently ushered her out the door.

"Okay, on the next landing, taxi her off the main runway and stop," Ethan directed as they did their third final approach of the morning.

They had been practicing takeoffs and touch-downs, and Julia shot him a quick, concerned glance because she thought she'd been doing everything by the book. "Is something wrong?"

"Not at all."

Not entirely convinced, Julia did as he directed. After completing her smoothest landing yet, she pulled off the runway and braked. But before she could ask him what was going on, Ethan released his seat belt and reached for the door handle. "What are you doing?" she cried.

"Don't shut her down," he said, seeing she was already reaching for the throttle. He cupped his hand beside his mouth and added, "Take her up and do the exact same thing again."

"Alone?"

"That's the idea."

"But I can't."

"Of course you can. You just did it."

Horrified, Julia watched him jump out of the plane. "Ethan, wait! I'm not ready to solo. I— I feel ill. I meant to tell you before we took off. It must be the virus that's going around."

"You're not going to make a liar out of me, are you?"

"What do you mean?"

"I told the guys that you'd be soloing today," he shouted, jerking his head in the direction of the main office. "And that you've evolved into one of the brightest students I'd ever had."

It was the nicest thing anyone had ever said to her. This was probably not a good time to ask if the guys in the main office knew, as she did, just how many students Ethan had taught. "I guess—" She had to swallow the lump in her throat to speak. "I guess I could try it," she managed shakily.

"That's a girl. You're a real trouper." With a parting wink, Ethan slammed the door and backed away from the Cessna.

Julia watched him, wishing he'd said something a little more personal, a little more romantic. One of them had to have lost his—or her—mind. There was no way she was going to solo. Right now it was debatable whether she could even take off! Everything Ethan had ever taught her had suddenly vanished from her mind.

She would probably crash. Who would tell the FAA that it was all *his* fault for sending up a student before she was qualified? Would they take away his license? Put him in jail? Too bad Texas prisons no longer put their inmates on chain gangs.

"Hey there, Cessna Three Five Alpha. Gator Tower, here. Whatcha doing, Julia? Writing your last will and testament?"

Gritting her teeth, Julia grabbed the mike and keyed it. "Kenny Spivet, that is *not funny*."

"Aw, I'm only teasing. You take your time. Don't feel pressured to take off until you're good'n ready. But, tell you what— I get off at six this evening and if you want, I'll drop by your place to tell your daddy he may want to have dinner without you. Gator Tower, out."

That did it. She'd show him...she would show them all. With a last glance toward Ethan, who still stood watching and waiting, she keyed the mike. "Gator Cove Unicom, Cessna Seven Seven Three Five Alpha is departing, Runway Two...*and I don't want to hear one more smart-mouthed remark out of you, Kenny Spivet*."

"Three Five Alpha, Gator Tower. Roger that. Have a good flight, Julia."

That was better. Julia replaced the mike, went through her preflight checklist again and taxied back onto the runway. Her insides felt as if they'd been bound and rebound in rawhide and the rawhide was shrinking. Droplets of perspiration trickled down her back and between her breasts. It didn't help that the runway suddenly looked about a mile too short.

Taking a deep breath, she adjusted the throttle, felt the Cessna push against the brakes and released them. "Oh, Lord," she moaned, feeling the rush of acceleration. Within seconds everything in her peripheral vision was a blur. "I can't believe I'm doing this!"

It wasn't, she decided, as she pulled back the wheel and left the earth behind her, as bad as she'd expected. Leveling off and beginning a right turn, she felt the suffocating grip on her lungs ease.

Relief brought laughter bubbling up her throat. She was soloing! *Really* soloing. It was incredible, and how much lighter the plane felt without Ethan's added weight!

She looked for him below but, of course, couldn't see him. Even the vehicles and planes were as small as dollhouse accessories. Scanning the sky, she spotted a fighter jet far in the distance. It was probably from the naval base in Corpus Christi, but she knew that it was on a different flight path and altitude and wouldn't interfere with her own.

By the second part of her turn—what she'd learned to call the downwind leg, which ran parallel to the runway—she'd already forgiven Ethan for pushing her into this. A twin-engine Beechcraft that had just announced its arrival landed. Julia gauged her position and called in her own intentions to come in.

When she had the runway before her, some of the tension returned. Takeoffs and landings, Ethan had told her countless times, offered the most challenging, dangerous moments for a pilot, and it was then that most accidents occurred. Determined not to become a statistic, she followed each step of the landing procedures intently.

The wind seemed to have picked up a bit, and the plane wobbled slightly. She compensated by adjusting the wheel to level the wings. Was this what gulls felt like as they approached the beach to hunt food? she wondered, easing the wheel inward, but feeling as if it was the earth that rose to meet her.

The Cessna made a hard landing and bounced slightly. With a muttered oath, Julia brought it back down. After dozens of landings she'd thought she had *that* technique down pat. So much for her lofty self-comparisons to a graceful bird.

Ethan wasn't where she'd left him, so she taxied the Cessna back to the hangar, where she found him waiting. The wide grin on his face brought one to her own and excitedly she shut down the engine.

"I did it!" she shouted, leaping from the cockpit. "I did it!" She ran to him, still feeling as if she were flying, then leaped to wrap her arms around his neck. "Oh, Ethan, I soloed and it was *wonderful!*"

He spun her around and around, his laughter matching hers. She was incredibly light in his arms, and her exuberance warmed him more than the sun did. It seemed the most natural thing to add a hug.

How her lips came to be pressed against his, however, was another thing entirely.

But surprised though he was, Ethan didn't waste much time wondering about it. The realization of how right it felt, how good it felt had already kick-started his heart into double time. Drawing back his head slightly, he stared down at her mouth. The impulse to taste it, taste *her,* made him draw in a sharp, needy breath.

"Open for me, honey," he murmured huskily.

"Ethan, I didn't mean—"

Taking advantage of her parted lips, he claimed her mouth with his, absorbing her startled gasp. Gently but firmly his tongue sought entry and discovered her sweet taste. When her own darted shyly to touch his, gnawing pangs of hunger prompted him to quench a deeper thirst.

Julia curled her fingers into the soft material stretching across Ethan's shoulders, vaguely aware that inside her jogging shoes her toes were writhing in similar response. In all her twenty-eight years, no one had ever looked at her, spoken to her, *touched* her with such sensuality. She couldn't believe what she'd been missing. She'd never thought of herself as sexy, let alone capable of feeling such cravings. Yet as her heartbeat grew urgent and her breasts ached to know more than the tantalizing feeling of being crushed against his chest, Julia realized that she really didn't know herself well at all.

A wolf whistle pierced the throbbing silence and thrust Ethan and Julia back to reality with the same reverberating shock waves Julia had felt when her feet once again made abrupt contact with the ground. Still so close that each breath brought them into sizzling contact, they stared at each other.

Ethan exhaled unsteadily. "I'm not sure which one of us is more surprised."

Julia knew exactly what he meant. Now that her head was clearing, she, too, couldn't believe that this had happened to *them*, of all people. "I'm sure it's only a fluke," she replied, though her voice hardly sounded convincing. It was as raspy as his. "The excitement of the moment."

"That's probably what it was."

"After all, we've known each other all our lives, and this has never happened before."

Ethan found himself tempted to remind her of the moment in his office several weeks ago, when he'd grabbed her. "Right. We don't even have anything in common."

"Except for the flying."

"Right, besides the flying. I'm not the kind of man you would...what I mean is, if you were—"

"No," she agreed quickly. "And I'm certainly not the type for—"

"No."

Somewhere inside her, Julia felt the last, flickering candle that was her euphoria go out, leaving her with a sudden urge to cry. Lifting her chin, she gave Ethan an overbright smile. "Well, then, there's nothing to worry about, is there? I—um— I have an appointment across town at noon, so I guess I'd better get going."

As she began to walk toward her car, Ethan called her name. Her throat ached terribly, and she was tempted to pretend she didn't hear him, but old habits were hard to break. She spun around. "Yes?"

"We forgot to do something. It's a tradition in the business. When a student solos for the first time, we cut off the tail of his or her shirt as a memento to hang in the office."

Julia lifted a hand to her top's wide, ribbed neckline. "This is new."

"Oh." Something in her eyes made him take a tentative step toward her. "I guess you can bring an old blouse or something next time. I only thought—" That was his problem, he warned himself, mentally gluing his feet where he stood. He was doing entirely too much thinking lately. Taking a step back, he told her there was no rush. "Bring something next time. It'll be fine."

It was a relief when she was gone. They'd been right to see how impractical, even foolish it would be to get carried away over one or two impulsive kisses, he told himself. No matter how pleasurable those kisses were. But as he walked back into his hangar, Ethan couldn't help but remember Julia's eyes and the wistfulness and disappointment he was certain he'd read in their depths. He had the most uncomfortable feeling that the memory of them would stay with him for a long time to come, even in his sleep.

Chapter Six

"**W**hat are you doing?"

Feeling like a convict caught in the crisscrossing beams of searchlights, Julia spun around. Her captor was standing in the kitchen doorway, buttoning the worn, short-sleeved shirt she'd been planning to add to the rag bin. Not exactly the stuff of high drama, Julia thought wryly. Still, his unexpected appearance had her hands shaking, and it took two tries before she successfully hung up the telephone receiver.

"Dad, you've been sneaking up on me all week!" she scolded, deciding that taking the offensive might hold him off long enough to make him forget what he'd asked her.

"Never you mind," Woody replied, craning his

neck from side to side. With a scowl that Julia couldn't decide was for her or the shirt's tight fit, he undid the collar button he'd just closed. "This is the second time this week you're canceling a lesson with Ethan, and I want to know why."

Julia thought of the excuse she'd used on Ethan. She told him she'd caught the "bug" going around town. At least he'd accepted it; of course, she had a feeling he would have accepted any story she offered. As for her father, who could see she was in perfectly good health, she knew better than to try that one on him. But could she explain Ethan's and her own unspoken decision to avoid each other?

"I'm just taking some time away from the flying, that's all," she said at last. Hoping to end it there, she gestured to his shirt. "Why did you take that out of the hallway closet? I was going to remove the buttons and cut it up for the rag bin."

Woody stroked a protective hand over the front of the shirt as if it were a beloved pet. "I like this shirt. Just because it's faded... What do you mean by 'time away'?"

"Exactly that. Taking two lessons a week has caught up with me, and I'm falling behind with other things."

"Like what for instance?"

"Like—my sewing. At the rate I'm going, I'm never going to finish that new dress I was making.

Remember? I sent away for the pattern in a magazine," she explained, seeing his skepticism. Warming to her story, she went to get the coffeepot from the stove and, carrying it to the table, filled his cup. "Then there's my vegetable garden. You know it takes an hour or two every evening to keep up with it. And *you* aren't interested in helping me."

"I have better things to do with my time than pull weeds and pluck bugs off bushes. Anyway, I've told you before, you can buy perfectly good vegetables at the grocery store."

Julia compressed her lips, but wasn't about to get into a discussion about what those *better things* were. It was one of the sore subjects between them, and she was in no mood for an argument. "Store-bought isn't the same thing. Besides, there's a certain sense of pride and pleasure that comes from eating something you've grown yourself. And before you sit down and get comfortable," she added, returning to the electric skillet on the counter, "I want you to know you're not going to Rocky's wearing that thing." Picking up the spatula, she methodically turned the sausage patties she'd been frying.

Woody plopped defiantly into a chair. "I'm not going to Rocky's, I'm going to Harlan's," he replied in a so-there tone of voice. "We're going to paint his garage."

"It's too hot to paint. Everyone knows you're supposed to paint in the spring or fall, otherwise the paint will blister and peel."

"Well, Ethan's been bird-dogging Harlan about it, so we're going to get it over with. He should be here any minute to pick me up. Have we made extra sausage, so we can invite him to join us?"

"Yes, Dad, *I've* made extra so *you* can invite him."

As if on cue, the sound of an approaching vehicle drifted through the screen door. Moments later Harlan Ross wandered in. "Morning, Julia," he drawled, beaming at her hopefully. "My, don't you look fresh as a posy this morning."

Her expression deadpan, Julia nodded to the table before turning back to the skillet. "Have a seat, Harlan." She added two eggs to the four in the skillet and scrambled them together. "Breakfast will be ready in a minute."

"Why, thank you. Don't mind if I do—but, er, only if you think there's enough." Winking at Woody, he sat down in the chair beside his friend.

Woody eyed him soberly over his coffee cup. "Julia's canceled her flying lesson with Ethan today."

"Oh? I'm sorry to hear that."

"She's decided she's falling behind on her chores."

"*Oh.*" Casting a furtive look at Julia's back, Harlan pantomimed a question to Woody. When Woody shrugged and shook his head, Harlan cleared his throat. "Well, Julia, it doesn't show. Why, I was just thinking as I pulled in the driveway, that Julia sure does keep a fine yard. And I'm not the only one who thinks so. Everyone talks about it. Yes, sirree."

Having withdrawn the sheet of homemade, baking-powder biscuits from the oven and prepared two plates, Julia carried the men's breakfasts to the table. She set each plate down with a thud. "Thank you, Harlan. I can't tell you what it does for me to hear you say that. Here's your coffee," she added, bringing him a cup of the steaming brew. "Now, if you gentlemen will excuse me, I'm going to go hang out some laundry. Did you know I'm also famous for my fresh-smelling sheets, Harlan? The secret is to let them line-dry. No short cuts with a dryer for me."

The two men lowered their heads to their plates and concentrated on eating until they heard her go out the utility-room door. Then Harlan dropped his fork and leaned across the table toward Woody. "Did you hear that? That was sarcasm in her voice. Wasn't she being sarcastic?"

"You *were* spreading your compliments a bit

thick, Harl,'' Woody replied, using the same loud whisper.

"Hmph. It's getting so that it doesn't pay to be sociable these days. What the heck's happened?"

"Your guess is as good as mine. Has Ethan said something to you?"

"He's said too much. Been nagging my ear off about one thing or another for the past week. Should have known it was because of something between him and Julia. You know what I think? They've had another fight."

"That's no reason to take it out on us," Woody replied gloomily. With a sigh, he poured extra honey over a biscuit. "I should have listened to you, Harl. This plan isn't gonna work."

Looking mournful himself, Harlan reached for his coffee. "Things were looking good, too. Why, Julia no more'n got those contact lenses and started wearing a little rouge, when Ethan began behaving different. Caught him staring at himself in the mirror several times now...even trying to see how he looks with his hair combed different."

"No!"

"Cross my heart and swear on the family Bible."

"Harlan, you don't have a family Bible."

"If I had one, I'd swear on it," Harlan replied, dismissing the technicality. "The point is that I think we've made progress, so this is no time to quit.''

"But what can we do?"

"We need to come up with another plan."

"It better be a whopper, 'cause I don't think Julia wants to be anywhere near Ethan."

"We'll have to figure out something so that she won't have any choice." Harlan picked up his last biscuit, sliced it open and tucked in his last sausage patty. "Hurry up and finish your breakfast, and we'll go over to Rocky's and work it out."

"I thought we were gonna paint your garage?"

About to take a bite, Harlan eyed him from beneath his bushy eyebrows. "Woody, we're talking about our future here. Do you really think this is the time to worry about a little peeling paint?"

Julia spent the rest of the morning trying to keep herself busy and her mind off her troubles by attacking the chores she liked to do least. Finally, after washing and waxing the kitchen floor, she took out the sewing she'd told her father about.

Actually, the white eyelet, full-skirted dress was almost finished, lacking only the proper hem. Deciding that she needed to see it on in order to tell how much to allow for, Julia slipped out of the skirt and blouse she'd been wearing and drew on the dress. Then, turning around so she could see herself in the full-length mirror on her bedroom door, she considered her reflection.

She had to admit it was pretty. The scooped neck showed off her skin and seemed to emphasize the ash highlights in her brown hair. It was the kind of dress to wear going dancing, followed by a moonlit stroll around a pond.

Julia sighed inwardly. Fat chance of either of those things happening to her. In fact, she was beginning to feel as if it had been a waste to even bother sending away for the pattern.

"Oh, darn you, Ethan Ross!" she cried at her reflection. "I was perfectly happy until you confused everything."

But even as she said that, Julia knew she wasn't being fair. After all, *she*'d kissed Ethan first. It was a mere technicality that her kiss had been an impulsive gesture motivated by euphoria.

His kiss, however, had opened her eyes to a whole new spectrum of feelings. That was what had made it doubly hard when he'd backed off as if she were poison ivy, or worse. Acting as though it had been nothing out of the ordinary had been the only way she could think of to maintain a modicum of self-respect.

She was never going to be able to look him in the eye again, and that was all there was to it. She certainly couldn't take any more lessons—a major disappointment, now that she'd come to enjoy them. But the sacrifice had to be made. She was certain Ethan would be relieved to see the last of her. It wouldn't even surprise her if he changed his mind and refunded the rest of her money.

When she became aware of the sad expression on her face, she twisted her lips into a bitter smile. "Why so glum? It's what you wanted in the first place, wasn't it?"

The princess-style phone on her bedside stand rang, stopping her from replying to that. Calling herself a fool for being reduced to talking to herself, she padded over in her bare feet to answer it.

"Julia? That you?" Harlan wheezed upon hearing her unenthusiastic greeting. "I think something's wrong with the phones. Oh, Lordy, what else is going to happen?"

"Harlan, slow down," Julia replied, frowning as she sensed a definite panic underlying the man's voice. "What's going on? Has something happened to Dad?"

"You've gotta come over quick. Maybe you can convince him to go to the hospital."

"Oh, my—he's been hurt? Is he bleeding? Is he conscious? Have you called for an ambulance? Call for an ambulance, Harlan, I'm on my way!"

As soon as she hung up, Julia headed out of the bedroom, only to backtrack to grab her purse, then

again to slip on flat-heeled sandals. There was no
time to change, she told herself after a slight hesitation, when she remembered what she was wearing.
Digging out her keys from the side of her bag, she
raced down the hall and out of the house, slamming
the door behind her. She didn't even pause to dou-
ble-check whether it was locked or not. What did
security mean at a time like this, when your father
was injured…perhaps seriously…perhaps—?

"Stop it!" she whispered, sliding into her car and
fumbling with the simple mechanics of getting the
key into the ignition slot. She wouldn't think neg-
ative thoughts. He would be all right. He had to be
all right. She'd been so waspish to him these last
few days; she had to have a chance to make up for
that.

The Ross homestead was less than two miles from
their house, and Julia had never covered the distance
faster. As she veered into the driveway of the older,
ranch-style house, she frowned because there was
no sign of Harlan's station wagon. The ambulance
couldn't have beaten her here. But perhaps Harlan
had succeeded in getting her father into his own car,
after all, and was already on his way to the hospital.

Spotting Ethan's Jeep, she felt an instant's hesitation, but quickly dismissed it. Ethan would probably have gone with them to help. Just in case, how-

ever, it wouldn't hurt to check around to make sure that was what had happened.

As she climbed out of the car, Julia scanned the garage, which was separate from the house. There was no sign that the men had been painting, no ladder or any of the other paraphernalia that went along with the task. What was more, the siding was still the grayish-white, peeling disaster it had been for several years, so that canceled out the thought that maybe they'd completed the job.

"Dad? Harlan?" she called, heading for the house. She peered through the sliding, screen door before letting herself into the living room. "Dad?"

It had been years since she'd been in here, and it was like stepping back in time. Nothing had changed much; there were still the half-finished projects, the uncompleted living-room paneling, the partially painted kitchen cabinets.... But everything was relatively clean, Julia realized after a moment. Whichever Ross played housekeeper, he deserved more credit than she'd ever given him.

"Anybody home?" she called after checking the kitchen. She started down the hallway, checking one room after the other. Suddenly the door at the end of the hall opened, and Julia clapped her hand to her mouth to muffle a scream.

"What the hell—?" Still dripping wet, Ethan

grabbed the slipping towel around his waist and stared back at her with equal surprise. "Julia."

"I'm sorry. I—I knocked, but there was no answer," she mumbled, gesturing behind her. She looked to the left and looked to the right and quickly came to the conclusion that the hallway was too confining a place to have a conversation with a half-naked man. "If you'll just tell me if they've gone to the hospital—"

"They? Who?"

"Our fathers. Harlan phoned a few minutes ago. He said Dad had been hurt and I was to come right over. I can't understand how I could have missed them."

"I only just got home myself, but I haven't seen anyone."

Mystified, Julia shook her head. "I was sure he said they were here. They were going to paint your garage."

"Yeah, right."

"Ethan, this is no time for sarcasm. My father could be lying hurt somewhere, and I need to find him."

"Okay," he replied, immediately contrite upon seeing her concern was real. "Let me get some pants on, and I'll help you look around."

Trying to keep her gaze at least above chest level, Julia mumbled something inane and spun away to wait in the living room. Once there, she pressed her hands to her stomach and took a deep breath, embarrassed that when she should be concentrating on her father, her mind seemed intent on doing a full review of Ethan's physique.

Mercy, he was—built. It was unsettling to be reminded that the majority of that brawn was toned muscle. When they were younger and he'd teased her to the point of tears, she'd soothed her hurt feelings by calling him a big lummox. The description couldn't have been more inaccurate.

He'd looked awesome just now, standing there with water dripping in haphazard patterns from his hair and broad shoulders. Some droplets disappeared into the russet forest of hair that matted his chest, some ventured intriguingly over his pectorals to the taut plane of his belly, where they were eventually absorbed by the towel. Her fingers twitched spasmodically as she remembered the fleeting, yet compelling urge she'd had to trace their path herself.

"I didn't see any sign of them from my bedroom window, but let's check around the house, just in case," Ethan said, striding into the room.

Julia spun around. Her cheeks went from hot to burning with embarrassment. Well, he'd specifically said pants hadn't he? And that was exactly what he'd put on. It was *all* he'd put on. The jeans were faded and ragged, but what made them border on the outrageous was that he hadn't bothered to do more than zip them up. Dragging her eyes away, she could only nod and follow him out the door.

They circled the house and scanned distant neighbors' yards, but there was no sign of Woody or Harlan. When Ethan suggested they go back inside, Julia followed, feeling torn between frustration and anxiety.

"They must have gone to the hospital, after all. May I borrow your phone to call and find out?"

"Sure, but— Julia, are you certain it was my father you spoke with and not a prankster?"

"I know Harlan's voice as well as my own father's, Ethan," Julia muttered, reaching for the yellow pages on the bottom shelf of a side table. Finding the hospital's emergency number, she quickly dialed. But when she reached the admittance nurse, she was briskly informed that there had been no emergency arrivals since early this morning. "I don't understand," she said, sinking onto the edge of the couch.

"Give me that," Ethan said, already easing the phone out of her hand. He leaned over and dialed another number from memory. Seconds later he said, "Rocky—hi. Listen, by any chance is my father there?" He shifted his eyes to Julia. "Uh, yeah, maybe that is a strange question. Would you put him on, please?"

"You mean they're *there*?" Julia squeaked.

Hearing his father come onto the line, Ethan held up his hand to signal her to wait. "Dad—what's this about Woody being hurt...? What do you mean, you don't know what I'm taking about? Julia says you called her a while ago and told her there'd been an accident or something when you were painting the garage.... Uh-huh, painting... Dad, you wouldn't be handing me a line of bull, would you...? Okay, okay, but it sure seems damned peculiar.... No, that's all right, I'll handle it. See you later."

As he hung up, Julia decided she didn't like the look on his face, and *definitely* didn't like the side of the conversation she'd heard. "What's going on?" she asked warily.

"He says he didn't call," Ethan replied, placing his hands on his hips. "He says he and Woody have been playing cards at Rocky's since about ten this morning, after deciding it was too hot to paint. The only accident he knows of is the bottle of beer Rocky dropped. I think," he added with a dangerous softness, "you better tell me why you're really here."

"What?" Julia's eyes went wide, and one of her contacts began to pop out, only to slap back against her eye when she blinked. "Ow!"

"Are you okay?" Ethan said, bending to see why

she was ducking her head and covering her face with her hand.

After several blinks, she recovered enough to lift her head and, through lingering tears of pain, shot him a murderous glare. "No, I'm not all right, I'm furious. You think I owe you an explanation? You think I would come over here in a half-sewn dress— that I would come here at all—if I didn't believe it was an emergency?"

Ethan's answering smile held all the confidence of a man who was familiar with being chased. Yes, he'd noticed the dress and thought it was a clever touch. "I'll give you an A for creativity, honey, but the game's up. I'm on to you."

"Ooh!" she exclaimed, seething, jumping to her feet and pushing at his chest in an attempt to move him out of her way. "Let me out of here before I say something vulgar, but exceedingly accurate, in describing my opinion of you, Ethan Ross."

But Ethan had no intention of letting her get off so easily. With a throaty laugh, he gripped her wrists, securing her against him. A moment later he realized his mistake. The feel of Julia's hands on him was just a reminder of how good it could be between them. Her touch sent tiny needles of aware-ness and need through his body and sharpened his appreciation of the view he had when he looked down into the gaping neckline of her dress.

He lifted his eyes at the same time she did. Their gazes met and clung. Seeing the shock in her own eyes turn to unmistakable desire, he stroked her wrists with this thumbs. "It's all right," he murmured at last. "I understand now, and you don't have to say anything else. I can take it from here."

With that he stooped and lifted her into his arms. Julia couldn't believe it. She was even more incredulous when he strode down to his bedroom and laid her across his bed.

"Ethan...wait!" she cried as he lowered himself over her. Then he covered her mouth with his, ending all chance for argument or explanation.

She'd never felt a man's body this intimately before; it made her tremble with excitement and not a little fear. She was aware of all of him at once, his powerful thighs, the pounding of his heart, the undeniable swelling behind the zipper of his jeans, his tongue, tempting her to abandon her inhibitions and join him in sensual love play. She wanted to—already her body was acting separately from her mind, her fingers exploring the forest of springy hair covering his chest, her hips shifting restlessly to sate some indescribable hunger. Her tongue was seduced by the slow, enticing strokes of his and offering its own invitation.

"I've been wanting this from the moment we kissed last week," he told her with a sigh, releasing her lips long enough to taste the creamy softness of her arching neck. "You went straight to my head, and I haven't been the same since."

"But Ethan, we need to talk."

"Why? Talking always gets us into trouble. Don't you think we communicate better this way? God, you're sweet. I want to unwrap you and taste you all over."

His raspy voice, as much as what he was saying, made Julia's body tingle with excitement. "There was a time when you'd say I was more like a sour lemon."

"That's because I wasn't taking time to see what was beneath that prickly shell you hide behind. We should thank your father for thinking of those flying lessons. If it wasn't for him, we might not ever have realized how compatible we can be."

As he explored the line of her collarbone with his lips, the impact of his words hit Julia like a blow. "Oh, my God!" she gasped. "Ethan!"

The combination of her cry and the way she was thrusting at his shoulders made him rise onto his forearms. "What's wrong?"

"It's all been a setup. Why didn't I see it before? That phone call from your father, the lessons from mine—our parents have been manipulating us. Trying to get us interested in each other," she explained, when she saw he wasn't following.

He considered that for a moment and then offered her a wry smile. "Okay. Then I guess they succeeded."

As he began to lean close for another kiss, Julia twisted her head away. "Is that all you can say? They stick their noses into our lives, trying to play matchmaker, scare five years off my life, and you're not upset?"

"I think the important thing at the moment is what's between us. I want you, Julia, and—okay, maybe you didn't come over here under false pretenses— No, don't interrupt," he said quickly. "Let me finish. What I'm trying to say is that there's a helluva attraction between us and nothing you can say is going to change that."

"You think that's enough reason for me to hop into bed with you?"

"It's served civilization pretty well so far."

Wanting nothing more than to curl up into a tight ball and cry, Julia turned her head away so he wouldn't see her hurt. "Well, thank you for those pearls of wisdom, Ethan. Now, if you wouldn't mind, I'd like to get up."

After staring at her intently for a moment, Ethan rolled to her side. "What was wrong with what I said?"

"Wrong? Maybe nothing. But for your information, Ethan, I'm not interested in a quick roll in the hay, or even a sizzling affair with someone who obviously thinks as little of me as you do.''

"Damn it, Julia, that's not true. Hold on a minute,'' he demanded, sitting up to grab her wrist before she could get completely away. "I think a lot of you. You believe what just happened on this bed can be faked? How am I supposed to let you know how I feel if not that way?''

"*Romance,* Ethan. Courtship. Wooing. Ever heard of the words? It's when you take a little time to let a woman know she's special. It's inviting her out for a dinner or bringing her a flower or calling her, just because she was on your mind and you needed to hear her voice. It might seem ridiculous and old-fashioned to you, but I believe in those things.'' She laughed briefly, aware that the sound was more like a sob. "You want to hear a good joke? I'm one of the dinosaurs, Ethan. A real, live virgin, who thought it was worth saving myself for the man I'd marry. Until you kissed me, I wasn't even tempted to change my mind. But what a disappointment to discover I could have been tempted to abandon something I hold so precious to someone who doesn't even have the foggiest notion of what I'm talking about.''

Hating herself for being unable to check the flow of tears that spilled from her eyes, and hating him for seeing them, Julia jerked her hand free and ran.

"Julia!" Ethan groaned, trying to stop her and failing. He heard the sliding screen door being opened and slammed shut and, exhaling his frustration, raked his hands through his hair. "You're wrong about me," he muttered to himself. "I just never thought...you never gave me a chance to...damn."

Chapter Seven

"**N**o need to ask how your weekend went," Bobbie Lee drawled, as she paused beside Julia first
thing Monday morning.

"Good. Then you won't." Though her co-worker
proceeded to perch herself on the edge of the desk
to finish a cup of coffee, Julia refused to look up,
instead continuing with the task of opening and sort-
ing her mail.

"Must have been a real bummer for you to go
back to wearing that stuffy old bun again."

"I like my hair this way, Bobbie Lee," Julia replied calmly. "It's easy to care for, yet sophisticated. Besides, my budget does not allow for weekly
trips to a salon like some people around here." This

time she glanced up long enough to give Bobbie Lee and her heavily sprayed curls a meaningful look.

Rather than take offense, the brunette patted her immaculate coiffure and grinned. "I just love it when you start sitting as if you're about to have tea with the Queen herself and talking real proper like. But you're not fooling me for a second. You're strung tighter that this new, long-line brassiere I'm wearing. Come on, Julia. I know it has to do with Ethan, and if there's someone like me available to share her wealth of experience, you should take advantage of it. We girls should stick together."

Momentarily forgetting the mail, Julia leaned back in her chair. "How can you be so blasé about something as personal as your private life?"

"Pooh." Bobbie Lee limply waved her hand. "It's not personal at all. What's the one thing all us women have in common? Men. And what's the other? The knowledge that deep down, men are nothing more than little devils, and that there's never been one born who can stay out of trouble for longer than a coyote can resist an open door on a henhouse."

Julia stared at her for several seconds before blinking and returning to her work. "I'm sure there was a grain of wisdom in that somewhere, but apparently it's too early in the week for me to see it."

The comment brought a pout to Bobbie Lee's lips.

"Are you or aren't you down in the mouth over something Ethan did or didn't do?"

"I wouldn't pay him the compliment of limiting my annoyance to him alone," Julia stated with a toss of her head. "I'm more than willing to extend my opinion to include the entire species."

Bobbie Lee nibbled on the edge of her plastic cup as she pondered Julia's remark. "The only thing I can make out of that is that Vern Culpepper must've escaped his mother's clutches long enough to make a pass at you."

"Bobbie Lee!"

"I guess not. Well, then stop beating around the bush and tell me what you're talking about."

"I'm talking about my father," Julia replied, despite her previous intention not to. "Do you know why he bought me those flying lessons?"

Bobbie Lee gave a feminine shrug before fluffing the ruffled collar of her blue and black, polka-dot suit. "To tell you the truth, Julia, I just figured he was getting a little ringy in his old age."

"Hmph. Ringy as one of those coyotes you mentioned. He and Harlan came up with the idea that it was time Ethan and I were married. And wouldn't it be convenient if they could get rid of two offspring with one ceremony, as it were?" The mere thought of the confession she'd finally wrangled out of her father Saturday night fired Julia's temper again. "I've never been so angry or so humiliated in my life."

Before Bobbie Lee could comment, the front doors swung open and a huge, funeral wreath walked in. At least that was what it looked like to Julia. It was at least four feet in diameter, and the evergreen boughs were trimmed with dozens of white carnations and a white satin bow.

"Who died?" Bobbie Lee asked, looking more miffed at the thought of having missed out on some news than concerned for the bereaved.

As the wreath made its way across the lobby and around the counter, Julia had two heart-sinking realizations; one was that everyone in the building was stopping work to watch, and the other was that the conspicuous thing was headed toward her.

"Hi, Miz Woods," a cheerful voice said, as the monstrosity settled onto four wire and two jean-clad legs beside her desk.

Julia looked up to see a dark head peeking around the right side of the wreath. "Tyrone...I didn't recognize you behind all that—ah—what's this all about?"

"Delivery for you."

"There must be some mistake."

"No mistake. Got a card."

"Oh, goody," Bobbie Lee said, wriggling off the desk and hurrying around boy and wreath to stand behind Julia, even as Tyrone handed over the envelope.

Too dumbstruck to protest, Julia took it and tore it open. She barely noticed the finely drawn yellow roses along the edge of the card; she was too busy reading the carefully printed message: "I'm mourning the loss of our friendship." It wasn't necessary to see the scrawled *E* at the bottom to know who'd sent it. Wondering if her cheeks were doomed to stay a scorched red, she quickly stuffed the card back into its envelope.

"Isn't that the cleverest thing?" Bobbie Lee cried, her voice peaking on a high C. Then, to Julia's dismay, she announced to all the onlookers, "It's an apology from Ethan on account they had a little spat."

"For heaven's sake, must you?" Julia whispered, mortified.

"Oh, relax," Bobbie Lee said, dismissing the rebuke with an airy wave. "If they don't already know, they soon would."

But Julia didn't share her co-worker's casual attitude. Feeling as if her back were going to snap, she turned to Tyrone, who was grinning unabashedly and looked in no great hurry to leave. "I'd like you to take this back," she told him, her voice shaking in her attempt to retain her temper.

"You don't want it?"

"Precisely. Tell Mrs. Jackson that I appreciate all the hard work she's obviously put into it, and that she has my permission to either donate it to one of the funeral homes or take it apart and send the flowers to the nursing home. I really don't care, as long as you get it out of here. *Now.*"

Mourning our friendship, she fumed silently as Tyrone mumbled a dejected goodbye to Bobbie Lee and carried the wreath away. What nerve! They hadn't even gotten as far as friendship. All they'd achieved was a beginning...a fragile beginning, which Ethan had ruined with his casual dismissal of her feelings.

Feeling worse than she had when she'd arrived that morning, Julia picked up her letter opener and brutally slit the next envelope.

Eventually some guilt seeped through Julia's anger and hurt. The wreath had obviously cost Ethan a small fortune, a fortune he couldn't possibly afford if he was planning on restructuring his businesses so radically. But she reassured herself by rationalizing that returning his gift would teach him a lesson he needed to learn.

Whether he would learn became questionable when on Wednesday Julia received another delivery. It was nearly her lunch hour and she'd just come out of Mayor Bainbridge's office, where they'd been reviewing some reports about to be sent off to Austin. As she walked toward her desk, her back was to the door, and she missed seeing Tyrone enter the building. Bobbie Lee's delighted whoop, however, soon had her doing an about-face.

"Oh, no!" she moaned, the instant she saw Tyrone's latest delivery.

He was carrying a teddy bear that, while not as huge as the wreath, required some juggling on his part to handle. She would have to have been blind not to notice that with its glasses and prim dress, the bear was outfitted to resemble her. But it wasn't the mimicry that had her crossing her arms, or the garlic lei around its neck that had her tapping her foot. It was the title of the book spread across its lap.

"Tried and True Ways to Fight off Unwanted Advances," Bobbie Lee read as she leaned out her payment window. "Why, Julia Woods, you sly thing! You didn't tell me that Ethan actually had gone so far as to make a pass at you."

Julia covered her face with her hands and wondered why she, a relatively decent, hardworking woman, had been chosen to be the object of all this persecution. Doing her best to ignore that comment and all the guffaws and giggles she heard around her, she splayed her fingers to peer at Tyrone. "Is there a card with this one?"

"No, ma'am. He said he reckoned you'd know who it was from."

"For once he's right about something," Julia muttered, scowling at the bear. Surely she'd never looked this—frumpy?

"Isn't it amazing?" Bobbie Lee gushed. "It's as if somebody made a miniature copy of one of your old dresses, Julia."

The smile Julia gave her could have frozen the Gulf. Then she turned back to Tyrone. "Take it back, please."

"Aw, Miz Woods. We're already one day late delivering this to you. Do you know what Miz Jackson had to do to find a whole string of garlic? I ended up having to drive all the way to the farmers' market in Corpus Christi! You're gonna break Miz Jackson's heart, if I show up back there with this."

He was right, Julia thought, nibbling at her lower lip. Just because she didn't want anything to do with Ethan Ross was no reason to upset everyone else. "Your little sister's still young enough to like stuffed animals, isn't she, Tyrone?"

"Yeah, but I know she ain't wild about garlic."

"Oh, I'll take the garlic," Julia replied, lifting the lei over the bear's head.

"What're you gonna do with it?"

"Knowing Julia, she'll probably chew a couple

of cloves next time she sees Ethan coming,'' Bobbie Lee announced before Julia could answer.

It was the final straw. Julia took the garlic and strode to her desk, where she snatched up her purse. ''I'm afraid you all will have to find someone else to provide your entertainment,'' she announced to her rapt audience. ''I'm going to lunch.''

For the rest of the week Julia was a nervous wreck, waiting in dread for the next delivery. None came, and by Friday she began to hope the silence meant whatever misguided impulses Ethan had had were over.

It wasn't until she was driving home Friday evening that she allowed herself to acknowledge that the wreath and bear had been—strange as they were—attempts at an apology. Until then she'd been certain he'd only been out to embarrass her in front of her co-workers. Still, it didn't change her opinion that she'd been right to refuse them, just as she was right to walk away from him when she did. They were all wrong for each other.

Saturday brought a new problem, namely her next lesson. Despite her change of attitude toward flying, Julia had no intention of continuing. The problem was, she also didn't want to call Ethan to tell him so. Granted, it wasn't the right way to handle things, but as the hour for her appointment came and went, she told herself it was worth it, just to avoid another argument with him. The man would eventually figure things out for himself.

It came as no surprise, however, that twenty minutes after the time of her scheduled appointment, the phone began to ring. Certain it was Ethan, she didn't answer it. Nor did she answer the call ten minutes later or the one three minutes after that. The fourth time the ringing didn't stop, and Julia, certain that she would lose her mind if the ritual continued, pulled the cord out of the wall.

By Sunday she was more than ready for church, hoping the discipline required for teaching a Sunday school class of seven-year-olds and the music and sermon during the main service would get her mind off herself. The class alone accomplished that. Though a few regulars were absent because of family vacations, the remaining brood made up for it by testing her patience and humor throughout the hourlong session.

Finally dismissing them, she spent some time visiting with other teachers and the Reverend Mr. Neely in the vestibule before settling in her favorite pew.

Soon the combination of organ music and the sun filtering in through the window had Julia smiling with contentment. When Mr. Neely asked the congregation to open their hymnals, Julia sang with an added zest, certain that she'd climbed her emotional mountain and had triumphed.

The minister was only moments into the sermon when her attention was drawn to two of her students, now sitting with their parents a few rows ahead of her. Though it wasn't uncommon for them to yawn or squirm during this part of the service, they were now blatantly disruptive. Julia frowned slightly when, despite their mother's whispered reprimand, they kept nudging each other and pointing out the window.

Moments later, the child behind them craned his neck to take a peek and then another, a few rows up. Good grief, Julia thought, glancing outside herself, what was the attraction? There must be a puppy or a stray cow from the neighboring farm wandering around in the parking lot. But except for a giant, gray crane standing in a stock pond several hundred feet away, she didn't see anything to justify the preoccupation.

Less than a minute later, Julia saw one of the deacons of the church glance out the window and do a double take. Then in the row behind him, a little girl pointed and said in a loud whisper, "Mommy, look!" It was impossible to ignore, and several people turned to peek outside. To Julia's amazement and consternation, they were soon smiling—worse, turning to smile at her!

What was going on? No longer able to concentrate on the Reverend Mr. Neely, who was having his own problems dealing with the disturbance, Julia finally heard the drone of an airplane overhead.

Her heart stopped.

He wouldn't dare. No longer caring about appearances, she swung around and, looking out the window nearest her, scanned the skies. "Good Lord," she whispered a moment later.

He dared. Ethan was out there, circling over the church in his stunt plane, which was bad enough all by itself. Compounding the situation, he was dragging a huge sign behind him like those aerial advertisements she'd remembered seeing on the beach as a child. But this message wasn't an advertisement. It was a message directed to her.

I'm Sorry, Julia!

Wanting to do nothing more than crawl under one of the pews and die, she turned back to the congregation, to discover that Mr. Neely had given up and was directing the organist to play a closing hymn. Julia didn't know how she got through it, but forced herself to sing with the rest. She was on the minister's heels as he exited the church to say goodbye to his parishioners.

"I'm so terribly sorry," she told him as he clasped her hand. "I don't know what's come over the man."

The pastor looked more amused than annoyed as he glanced heavenward. "Repentance would be my guess, Julia."

"I don't think so," she replied. "He's been pulling stunts like this all week, when all I want is for him to leave me alone."

Beside the minister, his wife Rebecca chuckled, a whimsical smile warming her eyes as she looked up at the plane. "I think it's wonderfully romantic."

Romantic? Julia stared at the woman in disbelief. A man embarrasses someone so that she can hardly bear to be seen in public, and it's considered romantic? Feeling totally out of sync with the world, she mumbled an excuse and hurried down the stairs.

Suddenly the entire exiting congregation gave a startled cry; dozens of wild roses struck them on the head, shoulders and arms. As women squealed and tried to protect children and hairdos, Julia dragged out a rose that had caught in her own hair.

The crazed man was dropping the things by the bucketful, and he hadn't even removed the thorny stems!

That did it. Gripping one flower between its thorns, she stalked to her car. The engine gunned to life under her impatient foot, and gravel and dust swirled when she backed out of her slot, then raced out of the parking lot.

She'd been willing to forget everything, but the

man was obviously intent on getting her laughed out of town! Well, she was going to stop this once and for all, she assured herself as she raced down the empty highway. Peering up through the windshield, she saw Ethan following like a homing pigeon. She uttered a growl between clenched teeth and floored the accelerator.

When she arrived at the airport, she drove to Ethan's hangar and was waiting with her fists at her hips when he taxied onto the grass to park. As soon as he shut down the engine, she was out of the car and heading for him. Murder glinted in her eyes.

"Oh, you've pulled some stunts in your time, Ethan Ross," she exclaimed, seething, even before he could climb down from the red biplane. "But this time—do you realize what you've done?"

Ethan jumped to the ground and turning, gave her a sheepish smile. "Apologized."

"Apologized? You practically maimed the entire congregation with that assault!"

Ethan drew his brows together. "They were only roses, Julia."

"Roses with *thorns*." His expression would have made her laugh if she'd been in a more receptive mood. "You didn't even consider that, did you?"

"Uh— I guess not. I was intent on making a point."

"Oh, you made a point, all right. In fact you made

several in just about everyone. Has it occurred to you that every person there is probably calling the sheriff to file a complaint? I'm surprised he didn't beat me here to arrest you.''

''He's not going to arrest me.''

''What you did was illegal.''

''Maybe it was, but he still won't arrest me when I explain to him why I did it,'' he shot back just as hotly. ''Damn it, Julia, I saw the people laughing and waving at me. Are you the only one in this town without a sense of humor? You wanted romance, I was trying to give it to you. Maybe it wasn't the way you expected it, but then I'm not exactly what you expected, either. I won't ever be. But I'm here and— I don't want us to fight anymore, so...'' He paused, realized he was practically shouting at her and finished quietly, ''What do you say?''

Julia didn't know what to say. He'd hit her with a few home truths she hadn't expected, ones she'd needed to hear. Her sense of humor, based on past experience, was rather narrow where he was concerned. That didn't make it right. He'd gone through a great deal of trouble and expense to apologize to her, more than many men would bother with. Instead of feeling flattered, she'd let her foolish pride rear its head and had behaved as if they were children again. And she'd called *him* the child who'd never grown up?

Yes, he was right saying he wasn't what she'd envisioned when she thought of a man in her life, and she would be deceiving herself if she thought he would change totally. But did she really want him to? Could she deny that he made her feel more alive, more feminine than anyone she'd ever met?

Aware that she'd almost ruined the progress they'd made over the last several weeks, Julia dropped her gaze to her clasped hands. "I—guess I've been pretty unfair and rigid about all of this."

"I wasn't without blame myself."

"You were reacting to my temper, and it wasn't right of me to be accusatory to you for what was initially my father's fault."

"*Our* fathers'," Ethan pointed out wryly.

Julia, her heart fluttering in reaction to the appeal and tenderness she saw beginning to light his eyes, lowered her own shyly. "You shouldn't have spent so much money, especially when you're trying to start a new business."

"The idea was to get your attention."

"The bear was rather cute."

Heartened by that, Ethan reached into the back of his jeans, drew out a ribbon-adorned corkscrew and offered it to her.

"I'm afraid to ask what this is for," she murmured.

"It's to open the wine that goes with the picnic

lunch I have in my Jeep.'' He cleared his throat. "I thought...maybe if you didn't have anything better to do...well, it is lunchtime.''

Julia's smile widened. She'd never seen Ethan tongue-tied before and found that it was almost more irresistible than when he was trying to be nice. "Are you inviting me on a date with you?"

"I guess that's about the gist of it." But he immediately felt compelled to apologize. "The food's nothing fancy. I'm not the cook you are.''

"How do you know I'm a good cook?"

"Are you kidding? My father rubs it in all the time. He can't wait to get out of the house Saturday morning, when he knows you're baking biscuits and stuff. It used to rile me, but when I think about it now, I guess it was more envy than jealousy.''

"The next batch of biscuits I make, I'll send back extras for you.''

"That's nice, but—what about lunch?" Ethan asked, thinking that in her light blue dress with its wide, white lace collar, she looked like a particularly appealing confection herself.

Julia wondered how she was going to eat a bite with butterflies doing aerial dives in her stomach. Deciding she'd worry about it later, she smiled and nodded. "Yes, Ethan. I'd love to have lunch with you.''

Chapter Eight

"I thought we'd go to the lake," Ethan said after they were settled in his Jeep and backing away from the hangar.

The town lake was at the opposite, less populated end of town. The same stream that fed it continued to meander its way in a serpentine path until it emptied into the cove that was part of Copano Bay. Julia occasionally drove past the romantically scenic spot, but rarely stopped. She felt out of place among the couples and families who were the most frequent visitors. The realization that she was actually going to picnic there herself as someone's date gave her a feeling of quiet euphoria.

No, she corrected herself, as she turned to smile

at Ethan. Not someone's date, *his* date. "That sounds wonderful," she replied softly. She looked at him, really looked at him for the first time since he'd climbed out of the stunt plane.

His hair was still a windblown riot, but there was something different about him today. A moment later she realized it was his clothes. He wasn't wearing his usual scruffy *uniform*. Oh, he wore jeans, all right; these, however, were so new that they even had a pressed seam. But the T-shirt had been replaced with a green, blue and white plaid shirt. It might not be formal wear, but it was the most dressed up she'd seen him since he'd gone to his old grade-school teacher's funeral. Julia thought that if he'd meant to impress her, he had succeeded.

Sensitive to her study, Ethan self-consciously smoothed a hand over his hair and struggled to think of something intelligent to say. He would settle for anything interesting or witty. Funny how, despite knowing her his entire life, nothing resembling either quality was coming to mind. He was too aware that a great deal of ground between them needed to be reexplored.

"The wildflowers are especially nice there this year," he murmured, after abandoning a half-dozen other glib observations.

"Yes, I like to go there myself."

That made him frown. When had she been here?

With whom? The questions came etched in neon green. When he'd tried to think "romantic" and "new," this had been the best he'd been able to come up with. The picnic was supposed to be the cherry on top of the sundae, the icing on the cake. Did she know she'd just dropped a giant anvil, crushing both—*and* his hope of getting back into her good graces? "I see. If it's become old hat, we could always try somewhere else."

"Oh, no! I didn't mean— I've never been there for a picnic or anything. I just like to drive past on my way home from work to admire them." Too embarrassed to meet his gaze, she kept her eyes on the purse clutched in her lap, and added quietly, "You know, I've never dated much."

He was glad. She might still be a virgin, but that didn't mean there hadn't been those who'd tried to coax her into changing her mind. Call it foolish, call it macho, but suddenly he knew he wanted to be the one, the *only* one who lay down with her in the lush grass and discovered how sunlight tasted on her skin.

As the thought sent warm honey through his veins, he shifted in his seat. "This will be the first time I've done anything but fish there myself."

"In daylight, anyway," Julia murmured dryly, pursing her lips.

"Smart aleck. Okay, so you got me there." He

sighed. "But those days are long over, and what happened didn't amount to much more than some heavy necking."

"With Wanda Sue Carson?" She laughed softly. "Ethan, really. I may not have your experience, but I'm not totally naive."

The trouble with living in a small town, Ethan thought grimly, was that it made it damned difficult to keep any secrets. But before he could begin to explain or deny, he felt Julia's hand on his arm.

"It's ancient history, and I shouldn't have brought it up."

"No, you've a right to know. I may never have married, but I—well, I wasn't an angel."

True...and that was part of the reason Julia still couldn't quite believe that he would be even slightly interested in someone like her.

"Stop it." When out of the corner of his eye he saw her turn to look at him, he continued quietly, "Don't sell yourself short. Not with me or anyone else. I didn't ask you to come with me out of charity or guilt or any of the other dozen reasons you're probably fabricating with that fertile imagination of yours. I asked you because I want to be with you, and if you don't stop looking at me like that, I'm going to pull over right now and show you how much."

Though Julia did as he asked, she couldn't stop

the tremor of excitement that raced through her body. She wouldn't have protested if he *had* stopped; she wanted him to kiss her again, and it was shocking to realize she didn't care who saw them. Wisely, she thought, Ethan suggested they change the subject, and he began telling her how glum his father still was, because she'd taken to serving cold cereals for breakfast as punishment for both men's meddling. Soon they were laughing over their parents' childish pouting, and by the time they arrived at the lake, she could even look at him without feeling a blush creep into her cheeks.

Ethan turned onto the narrow dirt road that circled the lake and, halfway around it, parked in a secluded inlet. The grass-covered ground sloped downward to the water, and a huge willow tree on the right offered privacy from the main road.

As Julia climbed out of the vehicle, she drew in a deep breath, enjoying the sweet smell of grass and flowers. Her flat-heeled sandals made only a whisper of noise as she walked toward the water to admire the bountiful daisies, black-eyed Susans and the smattering of stunning orange the butterfly weeds provided. On the left a huge mound of wild rose-bushes bloomed in pale pink profusion, and even from where she stood she could hear the buzzing and droning of bees and hummingbirds, busily at work collecting nectar.

But what made her smile with pleasure was the rowboat she spotted resting on the bank. "Oh, Ethan, look! Wouldn't it be wonderful if we could take it out for a ride?"

He straightened from the task of unfolding the plaid wool blanket he'd brought to spread on the grass. "That's why it's there."

She turned in time to catch the mischievous smile on his face. "This is yours! You were that sure of me?"

"I was that hopeful." As he approached her, he extended his hand. "May I assist milady aboard?"

Charmed, Julia put her hand in his, then almost withdrew it. "What about the alligators?"

"Aren't you the one who told me there weren't any?"

"That was because you were making fun of my petition. You sounded pretty adamant about them being here."

"That's because *you* were giving me a hard time. Plus," he added, squeezing her hand gently, "I was annoyed that you were going to dump me for Vern Culpepper."

"I really wouldn't have gone with him."

"You probably would have, but I forgive you." Tempted to swoop down and kiss her there and then, Ethan carefully spun her around by her shoulders and helped her get into the boat. If the lady wanted wooing, she would have wooing, not caveman tactics. Heaven knows, she needs some romance in her life, he reflected; he was beginning to acknowledge he did, too. But as he pushed the boat into the water and hopped aboard, he wished the timing was better. It was the one dark cloud that overshadowed all this; with his plans to start a new business, he was in no position to get too serious.

"Is something wrong?"

Ethan looked up from his rowing. "Of course not. Why?"

"That expression on your face. You're not going to tell me we might have to do some heavy bailing before reaching land again, are you?"

Reminding himself that now was a time for fun, not worry, he dipped his fingers into the water and flicked them at her. "Behave. I was worrying about you getting sunburned." It wasn't a lie. The scooped neckline of her dress exposed more of her shoulders than usual and reminded Ethan of her fair skin. To protect her from the sun, he turned the boat and rowed closer to shore, where they could glide beneath the branches of large oaks and an occasional willow.

As they floated along, propelled by Ethan's lazy rowing, Julia trailed her fingers in the water. "This is so nice," she murmured, watching a school of minnows dash for cover.

Ethan considered her thoughtfully. "It doesn't take much to make you happy, does it? I mean, you really like living here."

"Simple people have simple needs," she replied with a shrug. "Aren't you happy here?"

"I've never really thought about it. To me one place is as good as another. Sometimes I think about moving to a metropolitan area, getting a job with an airfreight line or something like that. But then I think about my father. It's not that he's old, but I don't like to think about living too far from him. You saw how the house looks, what with all his unfinished projects. If I don't go after him, to at least cover exposed wires or put up the new shingles on the roof after he's ripped off the old ones, I'd have to worry about the place burning down or both of us drowning in the next heavy rain." He grimaced and switched the oar into his other hand. "He says I nag worse than my mother used to."

Julia barely remembered the lanky, dark-haired woman who'd left her husband and son so many years ago in search of a better life. "Have you ever heard from her?" she asked gently.

"Yeah, she sent me a birthday card that first year she left. It came the same day my father's divorce papers arrived, so I scratched through the address and sent it back." At Julia's soft sound of sympathy, he shrugged. "Hey, it wasn't as if she really cared.

She'd probably just had a passing case of conscience. If she'd waited twenty minutes it might have passed.''

"You were deeply hurt. I'm sorry that I never saw that before. I'd always thought of you as tough, maybe even indifferent.''

Ethan held her gaze with his. "We've all got feelings. And we've all had our bad moments here and there. Big deal. Anyway, where's it written that life was supposed to be one big party?''

In other words, Julia thought with a sad smile, he didn't want to talk about it. Maybe it embarrassed him to admit his vulnerability. She wouldn't push him—at least, not now. "Tell me about the tour service. How're the plans coming?''

"Slow, even though I did find a buyer for the crop duster. Sometimes I think maybe this whole idea is out of reach.''

"Don't say that!'' In her earnestness, Julia leaned forward on her bench and hugged her knees. "The community needs the kind of growth you're trying to develop.''

"Maybe, but the community is also more than familiar with my reputation. I've never really given a hundred percent to any venture I've started. Besides that, there's all this damned paperwork you have to do, just to apply for a loan. My accountant did my financial statement, but now I have to put together a prospectus. I'm bad at keeping maintenance logs on the planes. How am I going to do a prospectus?''

"I could help," Julia said excitedly. When he lifted his eyebrows in that way that made her feel twenty-eight-going-on-nine, she glared back at him. "You know I could. I've handled a variety of reports for Mayor Bainbridge, and while I may not have a full business degree, I have taken some night courses that should help.''

"I wasn't doubting your ability, Mouse.''

"Then what?''

"Wasn't it only a few weeks ago that you all but called me a lost cause?''

"And you told me you had to be crazy to let my father get that gift certificate, because gnats would grow rubies in their navels before I learned to fly.'' When she saw his lips twitch, she reached out to touch his knee. "Ethan...people can be wrong about people.''

So it appeared. A few months ago he would have laughed if someone had told him he and Julia would be talking like this, but now, with her fingers burning a hole in his jeans, laughter was the last thing on his mind. It was only the certainty that he would probably knock them both into the water that kept him from reaching out and giving her a kiss.

"I'm getting hungry. Are you getting hungry?''

Without waiting for a reply, he turned the boat around and began rowing back.

Several yards away from land they struck something. As Ethan swiveled around to check one side of the boat, Julia checked the other. It was then she saw the coarse, dark creature disappear under the boat.

"Ethan! An alligator!"

He should have known better than to move too quickly; she shouldn't have tried to climb over the center bench and grab his arm. Before either could warn the other, the boat rolled over, tossing them both into the water.

There was just enough time for Ethan to push away from it and avoid being struck on the head. Down he went, intending to strike out immediately to search for Julia, but instead his arm wrapped around something long and slippery. The alligator!

Water rushed into his mouth. His lungs protested and his heart pounded. About to thrust the beast away, something telegraphed from his fingertips to his brain, and instead he ran his hand along the creature's length.

It was a log.

He kicked to the surface, spat out the foul-tasting, green water and gasped for breath. "Julia?"

"Ethan, get out! Hurry!"

"Julia, it's all right—"

She wasn't listening; she was swimming, crawling and otherwise dragging herself to land. Coughing to clear his lungs, Ethan followed.

His feet got mired in mud as he stumbled the last few feet to shore. Water sluiced from him as if he were one of those statues in the middle of those fancy birdbaths he'd seen in the front yards of stately Corpus Christi houses. He had to stop to drag up his jeans, because they suddenly weighed a ton and were tugging low on his hips. Then he almost fell again when Julia grabbed his arm and tried to haul him out of the water herself.

"Are you crazy?" she cried. "Move!"

"Julia, it's okay."

"It's not okay. That was a...it was a—"

He could understand her being short of breath; he was still having problems himself. "A log," he wheezed, trying to repress another cough. "A broken limb that probably fell off one of those dying trees during the last storm that blew through...a piece of wood...a giant stick...but not—under any stretch of the imagination—an alligator."

"Oh."

He cocked an eyebrow. "You needn't sound disappointed."

"Don't be silly, it's just—oh, dear." She clapped a hand to her mouth, ducked her head and mumbled, "I'm so sorry."

She didn't sound sorry. She sounded——he ducked his head, too, trying to see around the dripping-wet veil of hair hiding her face——as if she was about to burst out laughing. A moment later she did.

At first Ethan felt wounded. After all, there'd been a few seconds when he'd believed they were in serious trouble. But then her vibrant, lyrical laughter dissolved his indignation and seduced him. "Little idiot," he said, a grin spreading over his own face. "Sit down before your knees buckle under the weight of that wet dress."

It did hamper her movements, but, even while she tried to wring the moisture out of the full skirt, Julia stumbled to the blanket. She plopped unceremoniously onto one side and patted the other in invitation. "Come on," she called between chuckles. "Join me. Those jeans can't be much lighter."

As she dissolved into another spurt of laughter, Ethan shook his head and joined her. At least she was right about the pants; they were damned uncomfortable in their present condition. It was a good thing the sun was directly overhead and as hot as an oven. But a few seconds later, when she'd twisted her skirt until it was inches above her knees, he wondered if sitting near her was such a good idea. It made him notice too much——her great legs, for instance, plus the fact that the wet dress was accentuating every sweet curve of her body.

"I feel like a half-drowned rat," Julia groaned, shifting to squeeze some water out of her hair.

Enough was enough, Ethan thought as he watched her small breasts lift temptingly beneath the wet cotton. Already bending toward her, he murmured, "Correction, a drowned mouse."

Julia hadn't wanted to admit that she'd been waiting for this from the moment he invited her here, but as he brushed his lips against hers once, then twice, she felt relief spread and warm those parts of her that the sun couldn't begin to reach. When he did it again, she lifted her hand to touch his cheek. She'd never imagined he could be this gentle.

"Do you intend to watch me all the while I'm kissing you?" he whispered, his own eyes heavy-lidded.

"Would you mind?"

He placed a lighter kiss on each corner of her mouth. "Not…as long as you told me what you were thinking."

"I was thinking that I like you this way—very much."

"Wet?"

She smiled wryly. "I also think you like to be bad."

Though his amber eyes twinkled, Ethan shook his head. "What I like is to be with you. Please, continue."

"But you're also considerate." She lowered her eyes to his mouth. "And tender."

"Want me to show you how tender I can be?"

Julia moistened her lips.

This time his possession was far more deliberate, though no less careful. He suckled her lower lip and then probed deeper to taste the headier nectar within the sweet cavern of her mouth. She was sleek and smooth, and when her own tongue touched his in tentative invitation, her receptiveness made him sigh with pleasure.

"You like that," she murmured, feeling the strong thrumming of his heart against her palm.

Ethan rubbed his nose against hers. "And you like knowing that I do."

"It makes me feel strong, but weak—does that make any sense?"

With a subtle nod, he carefully pressed her backward until she was lying on the blanket. Resting on an elbow, he leaned over her and traced her cheekbone with his thumb. "I understand, though it's been a long time, Julia. I haven't felt this way since I was a boy."

"I wish I knew more about—"

He cut off her words by pressing that same thumb to her lips. "If I wanted experience, I could get it anywhere. Don't you understand? You make it all new again, Mouse. Special." He slid his glance downward, noting how her small breasts were already rising and falling with each shallow breath. "Maybe I'd better prove it to you. Hold on, sweetheart. This kiss is going to curl our toes."

Toes, fingers, nerve endings—no, Julia amended when she felt the sizzling power of his kiss surge through her. Her nerve endings weren't going to curl, they were melting, along with her brain. That was all right, though; she'd spent the first twenty-eight years of her life thinking too much, anyway, trying too hard, being too good. Ethan was showing her how much she'd missed. What was more, she wasn't self-conscious or embarrassed, because he made her feel that her inexperience was arousing.

Ethan sensed her acceptance and trust, and his heart seemed to swell in his chest to bursting point. In his business he was used to people trusting him with their lives, but this was different, something that made the gift more *precious*. The word echoed in his mind before he broke the kiss to catch his breath.

Yet even when he knew he should, he couldn't stop himself from touching her. With his lips he explored the graceful lines of her face, her short nose, the delicate arch of her eyebrows, the fragile shell of her ear. By the time he'd worked his way to the slender column of her throat, they were both short of breath and shifting restlessly in their attempts to achieve even closer contact.

"Tell me if I'm too heavy or if this is too much," Ethan suggested, solving the problem by insinuating his right leg between both of hers.

Julia felt the delicious tingles spread from her thighs to the tips of her breasts. "Ethan..." she said on a sigh.

"Good?"

She answered with her eyes and slowly took his hand. "Touch me here," she whispered, leading his fingertips to her breast. "I feel..." What was the word she was searching for?

"Achy." Oh, yes, he knew. It was the way he was beginning to feel all over. But it was such a wonderful ache, he thought, smiling when she made a purring sound as his big hand covered her completely.

"You're so warm."

"You're so small."

"Too small?"

"No, no. But compared to me..."

"I won't break." Then just as she'd hoped, he shifted his hand so he could trace his thumb over the taut peak of her breast. Moments later she felt his lips run along the line of her collar, until he came to where her heart fluttered desperately like a bird seeking freedom. There was no stopping the small sound of contentment that broke from her throat.

"It can be even better," he said gruffly, already reaching for the first button on her dress.

One button was released and then another, until all that hid her from his gleaming, hungry eyes was the lacy, blue bra she was wearing. Weeks ago when she'd started her makeover, Julia had decided to splurge on new, more feminine lingerie. Seeing the flare of desire in Ethan's eyes and the reverence in his touch when he reached for her made her forget every rebuke she'd given herself over her extravagance.

She wasn't conscious of actually unbuttoning his shirt, but when she slipped her hands inside and explored the hard planes of his chest, she knew she wanted to bring him the same pleasure he was bringing her. As she raked her short nails over his nipples, she reveled in the way his body shook in reaction.

"Julia—honey, do that again."

"I never imagined men were so sensitive there."

Ethan wondered if he could survive teaching her the other places where he ached to be touched by those inquisitive, graceful hands. One thing he was certain of was that he couldn't bear resisting the feel of her sweet breasts a moment longer. He deftly released the front catch of her bra. Just as smoothly he slid an arm beneath her and lifted her against him.

Julia wanted to tell him she thought he was wonderful, that she never wanted this moment to end and wouldn't stop him, no matter what. But he chose that instant to crush his mouth to hers, stopping her from doing anything but kiss him back. It was the most intense, intimate moment she'd ever experienced, and she clung to him, desperately wanting more, wanting everything he would give her.

Seconds later Ethan uttered a shocking epithet and withdrew. Then Julia felt herself snatched up and repositioned, so that she was sitting cradled between his thighs, with her back against his chest. "Fix your clothes, honey. We've got company."

Belatedly Julia heard the sound of an approaching vehicle and, even as she automatically began to do as he directed, she twisted to glance over both of their shoulders. A van parked some hundred yards away. No sooner did the engine stop than doors were thrown open and several children burst out, hitting the ground running. The branches of the giant willow offered some privacy, but Julia was still embarrassed.

Ethan was equally shaken, but for different reasons. He lowered his head and buried his face against her hair, her neck. "Oh, God, I'm sorry. I'm sorry."

"Don't. There are two of us participating in this, you know." However, when seconds passed and he failed to make any other comment, Julia began to sense that there was more to his apology than she'd first thought. Was he even referring to their being caught in a compromising situation? "Ethan?" she inquired warily. "What is it?"

"Do you ever wish you could take back—something you'd said or did?" he finally asked.

It was hardly the reply she'd been expecting, and her immediate response was to pull away. But before she could, Ethan tightened the hold he had around her waist. "Let me go," she demanded, her voice low and unsteady.

"No. Not until I explain."

"What's to explain? You're sorry you kissed me!"

"No! Yes—oh, damn. No. Never." He knew the answer was confusing, but it did succeed in making her grow still. "Julia, I never expected that we'd— that this would get so serious so quickly."

"Then why did you ask me here? Why did you fly over the church and send the bear and flowers?"

"All right." He sighed, knowing the stack of evidence against him without hearing her list it. "At least, not this fast. Hell, we'd been at each other's throats all our lives, you'd think it would at least take a few months before—"

"Before I let you undress me and offered you my virginity? Thank you for your honesty, Ethan. Now let me go."

"Stop it," he growled into her ear, his rigid hold stopping her from regaining her freedom. "I meant, I have no business being here with you like this. Stealing kisses, when I know full well I'm in no position to offer you anything near what you deserve."

"They weren't exactly stolen."

"You know what I mean," he replied just as quietly, as intensely as she'd spoken. "Anything I take from you is as good as a theft, because I have so little to give in return."

She closed her eyes. "All I ever wanted was your honesty, Ethan. You're not responsible for anything else. My decisions are mine to make."

"You think so? You have a father who, despite his actions lately, would expect me to offer you a ring and all the trimmings, if we made love. And what about the rest of the town? Could you handle everyone knowing you're having an affair with me? Because that's all it could be, Julia. I've practically put myself out of work. My future is iffy, at best."

"Your new business is going to be a wonderful success!" she cried.

"Maybe. Someday."

"I'd be willing to wait," she said, lowering her eyes. "If I knew—if I knew you wanted me to."

Love. She'd almost said, *If I knew you loved me,* Ethan thought, feeling the impact like a blow to the heart. He'd denied it, dodged it and wrestled with it, but he knew when he was beaten. Yes, he'd fallen in love with this frustrating, adorable woman. But it would be hell on them both if he admitted it. Already she was getting exactly the kind of noble ideas he was learning to expect from her, like waiting for things to turn better for him. And when they didn't, she would insist that she didn't need anything but him to make her happy. Hadn't his father told him about the similar way it had begun with his mother? And he knew damn sure *he* wasn't the noble type. Even if they agreed to wait, he doubted he could keep his hands off her.

"Don't set yourself up for a lot of misery, honey," he said gruffly. Unable to resist, he rested his forehead against her hair. "I want you, but it stops there. Here. Now."

Tears burned behind Julia's closed eyes. Feeling as if her life were being snuffed out just as it was beginning, she whispered, "Are you going to deny me your friendship, as well?"

Ethan winced and blindly groped for her hand, lying like a broken wing in her lap. "Is there still friendship to offer, Julia?"

She knew she had to be a fool. The day would undoubtedly come when she would regret this, but she nodded slowly. "If you want it."

"I want it."

Chapter Nine

Friendship, Julia learned quickly, wasn't always
what it was cracked up to be. In the best scenario—
the one she prayed she could have with Ethan—she
thought that spending any time with him would be
better than not seeing him at all. What she discovered was that being around someone you were falling desperately in love with could be painful, even
while it was wonderful.

In the weeks that followed, she and Ethan did
their best to visibly establish that friendship was all
there was between them, so that people who knew
them, as well as their parents, would stop the teasing
and innuendos, the questions and—most especially—the humming of the wedding march. Julia

resumed her flying lessons, and Ethan let it be known that his priority was to spend every waking hour concentrating on developing his new business.

To all appearances, and despite their fathers' continued grumblings, they appeared to be making progress. But inside Julia felt like an abandoned corsage, after a date failed to show up for prom night.

Hardly inclined toward melodrama, she kept telling herself how difficult it was to die of a broken heart. Even Juliet had needed her poison and Cleopatra her asp. Yet something critical *had* shriveled up inside her and *was* dying. All that kept her going from one day to the next was the knowledge that she could still talk to Ethan, see him, even touch him—if she was feeling particularly masochistic.

At night, when she couldn't sleep and paced around her bedroom, she chastised herself. If she had any sense or self-respect she would quit the lessons once and for all and avoid Ethan like the plague. Each time she started for the airport, her intentions were to do just that. Then she would see him, catch a glimpse of something hopeful, something undeniable in his eyes, and she was lost again. Her insistence on helping him with his prospectus, however, had to be grounds for committal.

It was the amount of paper continually spilling from his office wastepaper basket and his bloodshot eyes that got to her. She could see he was still having problems. When a few, discreet questions to the secretary of his bank loan officer disclosed that one week stretched into the next and Ethan had yet to come in for a meeting, Julia knew she couldn't stand by and not help, no matter how difficult it might be for her emotionally.

One morning after a flying lesson, while Ethan secured the Cessna, Julia used the excuse of needing to borrow his phone and hurried into his office. Sitting down behind his desk, she opened the bulging folder that contained all his notes, graphs and financial history. By the time Ethan came looking for her, she had eliminated most of the useless or redundant material and was drawing up a list of information he still needed.

"What do you think you're doing?" he asked wearily, standing frozen in the doorway.

"Helping." Later she would commend herself on the casualness of her reply. "Do you know you're only listing half your potential clients on this sheet? And on this one you didn't put down that you also have experience with air rescue."

"It was one crisis during a movie shoot, and the only reason I was in that chopper was because the pilot was a friend and every hand counted."

"That's not what your father told my father. Anyway, what's important is that you didn't panic under pressure. That's the kind of thing a bank looks for, beyond all the profit and loss figures. They want to know the type of character they're dealing with.... Are you going to buckle under with the first sign of problems? Things like that. Now, I have an idea.''

It was that simple.

It was that difficult.

As expected, Ethan did his share of protesting, but quickly realized she had valid points and eventually gave in. In the days that followed, she met with him several more times and elbow to elbow they worked, often until very late.

Last night they'd pressed on until midnight, but had finally finished. Ethan was prepared for his loan meeting.

When Julia rose the next morning, she felt as jittery as if she were going herself. Instead, she dragged her exhausted body from bed and stumbled to work, looking worse than when she'd had the flu last winter. Her eyes were red and swollen from too many hours on the computer they'd borrowed, so they could use the desktop publishing feature to give Ethan's prospectus a professional look. Her hair, though clean, hung limply, and the beige suit she'd dragged out of the closet made her skin appear anemic under the office's fluorescent lights.

Considering her recent attempts to make herself over, it wasn't surprising that her co-workers eyed her strangely and voiced concern about her health.

Eventually she did add some color to her cheeks and lips; however, at two in the afternoon when Ethan walked in, she still wanted to hide under her desk, so he wouldn't see her when she hardly looked her best.

He'd told her he would let her know how the meeting went, but she'd never dreamed he would actually stop by. After all, the last thing they wanted was for people to once again start getting the wrong idea about them. Yet as she forced herself to her feet and crossed over to the counter, she couldn't deny the pleasure that accompanied her embarrassment.

Unlike her, he looked wonderful, wearing a camel-colored sport jacket, dark brown slacks and a crisp, white shirt. The style, though still casual, lent him a sophisticated air, and when he responded to Bobbie Lee's purred greeting with a crooked smile, Julia felt a stab of jealousy. It didn't matter that she knew perfectly well that Bobbie Lee purred even louder at her own reflection in the ladies'-room mirror.

"Hello, Ethan," she said, conscious of the painful pressure in her chest that intensified with each hour they spent together. "This is a surprise."

"I guess it is. But I knew you would be wondering about—things. Anyway, you *are* on my way home." He glanced from her to Bobbie Lee, who smiled back innocently. Shoving his hands deeper into his pockets, he tilted his head toward the door he'd just come through and asked Julia, "Do you have time to take a short break?"

"Oh, stay," Bobbie Lee muttered, taking the hint and sliding off her stool. "I need to fix this chipped nail, anyway. Inez, honey—let me borrow your nail file. Mine's plumb worn-out."

In a rustle of satin polyester she sashayed away. Julia edged closer to the counter. "This might not have been a good idea," she whispered to Ethan. "You know what a gossip mill it can be around here."

"Sorry. I wanted to talk to you. I guess I didn't stop to consider how it would look."

It was a small gift, but one that Julia hugged to her heart. "That's okay. I probably would have done the same thing." Self-consciously she tucked her hair behind her ear. "It, um, went well, then?"

"Yeah. Good. Smoother than I expected."

"That's wonderful."

"Of course, it's too soon to tell if I'll get the loan or not. The application still has to be presented to committee."

"Of course, but Mr. Northrup liked your ideas?"

"He actually sounded enthusiastic."

"I'm so glad. It's going to work out, you'll see."

"If it does, a major part of the credit goes to you."

Julia had to lower her eyes, because she didn't want him to see how much his praise meant to her. He didn't need or want to be burdened by her gazing at him like an adoring puppy. "I was glad to have been able to help," she said quietly.

"Enough to have dinner with me?"

Her head came up with a jerk. "I don't understand."

"Look, maybe it's too soon to celebrate, but tomorrow you're doing your first long-distance solo, and remembering how nervous I was before I did mine, I figured the least I could do was help get your mind off it for a few hours and start to pay you back some for helping me out."

The solo—amazing how she'd almost forgotten about it. But even now it took second place in her thoughts; she was more preoccupied with analyzing his invitation. It wasn't a dinner date per se, it was payment for services rendered. Oh, he was being a gentleman about it, but he might as well have said he wanted the slate cleaned between them. That hurt so much, she wrapped her arms around her waist to ease the pain. "You don't owe me anything, Ethan."

"Don't you think we could both use the break?"

Maybe he could. What she needed was a good,

long cry and a longer soak in a steaming tub. "I appreciate the offer, but—"

"Don't say no. I already made reservations at the Pelican Inn."

The inn was the nicest restaurant between Gator Cove and Corpus Christi. Dark and intimate, it was hardly the kind of place two people would knowingly go when they were intent on keeping their relationship uncomplicated. Surely he knew that?

"Please," Ethan murmured, coaxing her with a smile.

Don't let me regret this, she prayed as she felt her resistance weakening. "All right. What time?"

"The reservations are for eight. I'll pick you up at seven-thirty."

At seven-twenty that evening Julia was in her kitchen, a towel wrapped around her waist to protect her mauve silk dress, as she tried to finish preparing her father's dinner. He sat at the table waiting. Neither of them looked happy with the situation.

"For weeks you've used every excuse imaginable to avoid eating at home," she said, grimacing as she dipped too deeply into the saucepan and scraped up some of the soup that had burned on the bottom. "I don't know why you had to choose tonight to suddenly change your mind."

"And I don't know why you had to make me

New England clam chowder soup, when you know I like chicken noodle,'' Woody replied, compressing his lips even tighter when she turned and he saw the low drape of the back of her dress.

''I told you— I didn't do my usual Friday grocery shopping on my way home from work, and this is what was in the pantry. *Maybe* if you would have called me, I could have warned you what was available and you could have eaten out with Harlan.''

''I'm not speaking to Harlan.''

''Since when?''

''Since today.'' When Julia failed to ask anything more and merely set his soup and tuna salad sandwich before him, he shot her a frustrated look. ''Don't you want to know why?''

''Can't this wait until tomorrow, when I get home from my lesson? I have to finish getting ready. Ethan's taking me out to dinner, and he'll be here in a few minutes.''

''I don't want you going out with him.''

''What?''

''His father is a self-serving, conniving old buzzard, and you know what they say about genetics.''

''Oh, Dad. You weren't worried about genetics when you were playing matchmaker, were you?''

''I was blinded by what I thought was sincere friendship on Harlan's part. Now that I've had my eyes opened, I see the error of my ways. Can you believe I actually shared my last can of C rations with that ingrate, the Christmas of '52?''

"Yes, Dad, I can. He was your best friend and he still is, no matter what silly thing has put you off. You two wouldn't know what to do with yourselves if you couldn't have one or two skirmishes a year— none of which, I might add, bear remembering. I just wish you would have timed this one better,'' she added, filling the burned pot with hot water and liquid detergent.

"I'll remember. He dumped me to drive Rocky to town, so he could get a free beer! A man remembers who his friends are.''

"Good grief, Dad, you act like you're married to each other. He has a right to some personal time away from you. Even married people respect the need to give each other a little space once in a while.''

"Hmph. I'll give him space, all right. As for you, young woman, you're not stepping out of this house wearing *that*.''

"Oh, yes I am,'' Julia replied, leaving the pot to soak and heading for her bedroom. There she snatched up her pearl earrings and the matching necklace that had been her mother's. Standing in front of her closet mirror, she put them on and turned slowly to inspect the results. If this didn't do the trick, she mused, nothing would.

On the way home from work she'd had a revelation: she was being a fool. Why should she let Ethan make all the decisions about what should come of their relationship? Granted, he had a right to his opinion, and she would even allow that it was rather sweet of him to want to protect her by keeping things strictly platonic between them. But that didn't mean she had to listen to him.

She hadn't asked to fall in love with him, but for better or worse, there it was. She *certainly* hadn't fallen in love with him because of what she thought he might be able to give her.

Knowing that if it was left in his hands, he would build on the wall he'd put between them, Julia had made a sharp U-turn and gone back to town, where she'd found this dress. She intended to take full advantage of this *friendly* dinner.

Hopeful, she smiled back at her reflection. She'd never looked better. The cold water she'd splashed onto her eyes had reduced their puffiness. Excitement had put a glow back into her skin. The only question remaining was, should she put up her hair or not? She shook her head and watched it swing over her shoulders and settle in gleaming waves. About to scoop it up off her neck, she heard Ethan's Jeep turn into the driveway. Too late now. Grabbing up her purse, she headed back down the hall.

"Nobody's home!" Woody shouted as Ethan came up the steps and knocked on the screen door.

"Will you behave," Julia scolded. She bent to kiss the top of his head. "I'll see you later. Don't wait up."

"I most certainly will!"

"I went through the same thing at our place," Ethan said in a conspiratorial whisper as he opened the door for her. Then, as she descended the stairs before him and he saw the deep cut of the back of her dress, the rest of his comment died on his lips.

"You would think after all these years, they'd have grown beyond arguing over the trivial," Julia replied conversationally.

"Uh—yeah. I mean, those two? Never." At the Jeep, he hurried to open the passenger door for her.

"Well, at least it gives us a temporary reprieve from their meddling."

She had to be kidding, Ethan thought. He shut the door and circled to his side. She wears a dress like *that* and expects him to feel reprieved? He climbed in on the driver's side. It took him two tries to secure his own seat belt, and he missed when he reached for the key in the ignition.

"Are you all right?"

"Sure. The sun's just in my eyes."

"It is blinding at that angle," she said, leaning back in her seat and carefully crossing her legs.

She'd never worn such high heels before in her life, and she didn't want to snag her expensive, sheer nylons before they even backed out of the driveway. "But it feels good, especially after being in an air-conditioned office all day."

Yes, Ethan could see that. In fact, he was beginning to wish the Jeep's windows were tinted, because he had a suspicion that the woman beside him was literally getting tipsy on sunshine. It was the only logical reason he could think of for her to smile at him in that beguiling way, and shift in her seat so her skirt slid up another inch.

Forgetting all his prowess in driving a standard vehicle, he shifted into Reverse and promptly stalled out. It was the first omen that he was in for a rough night.

The restaurant was only a twenty-minute drive away—unless you hit every red light through town, realized you were almost out of gas, and found yourself stuck behind a tractor trailer carrying a load of cattle that had decided room service was lousy and had opted to mutiny. Under *those* circumstances it took an hour. When Ethan and Julia walked into the Pelican Inn, they could tell by the crowd in the entry hall that their table had long since been given to another couple.

The hostess confirmed that, and though sympathetic, told them it would be at least thirty minutes before another table would be available. "There might be a few seats in the lounge," she told Ethan. "If you're interested in waiting there, I'll call when we have a table for you."

He was interested. He already knew his nerves wouldn't last five minutes if he and Julia had to stand like two spoons in an already cramped cutlery drawer. Thanking the hostess, he placed a hand at the middle of Julia's bare back, snatched it away and settled it on safer territory nearer her waist.

If the lounge was less crowded, it was only on the dance floor. Ethan counted himself lucky to find a seat at the bar for Julia, but because the stereo music was amplified for the Friday night crowd, he was forced to inch close to her, after all. After a few minutes of breathing in the shampoo-fresh scent of her hair and feeling her thigh stroke his every time she turned to speak to him, he felt as if he'd been introduced to a new, intimate form of torture.

"You didn't have to order mineral water, too," she said, resting her hand just inside his sport jacket as she leaned closer to speak into his ear. "I'm the only one who has to fly tomorrow."

True, he thought grimly, but he didn't want to be tempted to fly tonight. "I might have a glass of wine with dinner. That'll be enough." Glancing over her head, he spotted the man beside her, who made no pretense of indicating his interest. Ethan stared him down, not even aware he'd taken hold of Julia's wrist and was stroking the inside with his thumb. "I'm really sorry about the way this is turning out."

"Oh, don't be. I'm enjoying it. It's a new experience for me."

Anyone looking at her tonight wouldn't believe it, Ethan thought, glancing over to the dance floor, where couples swayed to the slow song that was playing. He knew she was waiting for him to ask her to dance, but he couldn't do it. He didn't want to be reminded of how good it felt to hold her in his arms. He didn't need the added torment.

But if he thought things would be simpler staying where they were, he found out otherwise when the disc jockey in the corner interrupted the song, to announce that everyone should clear the dance floor for a lambada demonstration.

"Lam what?" Julia asked Ethan, who, instead of replying, groaned and reached up to rub the back of his neck. A moment later she realized why.

The disc jockey explained that for those who hadn't yet heard of it, the lambada was the exciting, Brazilian dance that was the newest rage sweeping across the United States. As he introduced the two couples who were going to do the demonstration, they ran onto the dance floor, smiling and waving to the cheering crowd.

Julia thought the girls resembled cheerleaders in their short skirts and midriff-baring tops. The men wore satin shirts in white and black, unbuttoned to the waist and tucked into pants that left little to the imagination. But her education didn't stop there. As soon as the music started, she got a crash course in body language.

"Oh, my," she breathed, only seconds after they began to dance.

Though Ethan had known what to expect, he found himself reaching for his mineral water to wet his suddenly dry throat. A few weeks ago one of the news shows had done a story on the dance and he'd been amazed then. But seeing a demonstration in person made it twice as incredible.

As he watched one couple's hips swing and rotate in unison, he decided he would have to have ball bearings put into his joints before he could achieve such an effortless-looking, fluid swing. No wonder people from Latin-speaking countries were typecast as being hot-blooded. He was merely watching, and his blood was already near the steaming point.

It wasn't healthy for the imagination, either. He didn't consciously intend it to get out of hand, but before he knew it, he could picture himself and Julia out there, pelvis to pelvis, thigh to thigh, their bodies swinging with every beat of the music. He didn't know what drew him, but he turned to look at her, only to discover she was already watching him.

The music receded, but the moment grew more intense. Ethan felt awareness sparking between them like two live wires held a hair's width apart. Then, as if he'd been pushed off a cliff, he found himself descending toward her in slow motion. The scent of her swam in his head, intoxicating him. The remembered taste of her lips and tongue was making his tingle, deepening the excitement and anticipation of what would be, what he was waiting for, craving. Another inch and it would no longer be a memory.... Another heartbeat and he would—

"Mr. Ross? Excuse me, but there's a table available, and we're giving you priority seating if you want it," a voice said behind him, jerking him back to reality.

He saw Julia close her eyes and understood. He felt like hitting something hard himself, but somehow both of them managed to obediently follow the hostess. They were shown to an intimate corner table that was lighted by only a single candle in its center. After the hostess handed them their menus and their waiter stopped by to introduce himself, they were once again alone.

"I wonder if I'm doomed to spend the rest of my life apologizing to you," Ethan murmured bitterly.

"Don't be silly." Julia couldn't yet risk meeting

his eyes and settled for concentrating on the way he was gripping his menu. "I'll admit the dance was suggestive."

"It was practically X-rated."

"Well, it's not like we were the ones doing it."

"No. I was only kissing you with my eyes. And instead of telling me to go to hell, you were kissing me back."

This time Julia raised her eyes to let him see the longing still shimmering there. "What did you expect?"

Candlelight caressed her lips and cheekbones, as he yearned to do. "It's not what I expect. It's what I want you to do for me...for both of us, whenever I forget my own rules."

"I'm afraid I can't," she whispered, lowering her gaze. "It wouldn't be honest."

"Julia—"

"Bobbie Lee is always talking about how good the shrimp cocktail is here. Remind me to tell you a funny story she told me about seeing her first live shrimp when she was a child. But right now, I think I'd like to start with that."

Ethan discovered just how tenacious Julia could be. As she'd clearly intended, she took control of the conversation and, just as she had done with her attire, set out to seduce him with what he was certain was her first attempt at impersonating a coquette. Ethan wasn't fooled by the act for a minute, but that didn't mean he was immune to it. By the time they were driving home, if he hadn't already been crazy about the woman, he would have been falling hard. That was why, the closer they came to her house, the more he started talking about things she needed to remember for tomorrow.

"You might want to pack a thermos or some gum. After San Antonio the terrain gets pretty boring, and I don't want you falling asleep up there."

"I won't fall asleep."

"Also, bring your glasses along, just in case. You never know.... You could lose a lens or get something in your eye."

"I'll bring my glasses."

He went into an involved description of the latest weather report he'd heard on the early-evening news. It got him all the way into her driveway. "Oh, and wear comfortable clothes. Being in that plane will be like sitting in a hot box."

Julia pursed her lips and shot him a sidelong look. "So I shouldn't wear anything as confining as, say, this."

"That's, er, not exactly confining—exactly."

"I didn't think you'd noticed."

He exhaled slowly. "I noticed."

"You could have said something," she replied

softly, abandoning her teasing to gaze at him entreatingly. "All I wanted to do tonight was please you."

Helpless not to, Ethan reached for her and grasped her upper arms. "Will you stop! You want to hear it? All right— I was pleased. I was attracted. Hell, I ache!"

"Then show me," Julia whispered, her fingertips grazing his jaw. "Kiss me, Ethan. It's all I want."

"No way, because we both know it's not what either of us would settle for. What's between us is combustible, honey. But it's no match against the realities of the tough times that are in my future."

"Ethan, look at me. Do you see a tiara on my head? I don't care if you don't have—"

"I *do* and that's the end of it."

As he released her, Julia slumped back in her seat. "How I wish I was beautiful," she said almost petulantly. "I think I'd make you grovel."

Ethan smiled despite the hunger still pulling at him. "Stop fishing for compliments, Mouse. You know you do just fine the way you are. Now be a good girl and get inside, wash off that war paint and get a good night's sleep. I'll see you in the morning."

"Silver-tongued devil," Julia muttered, getting out of the Jeep and feeling anything but agreeable. "Maybe you will see me and maybe you won't."

"Tomorrow," Ethan said, his voice a low rumble in the darkness.

How could she fight him when he beat her at her own tricks? she fumed, slamming the door and scowling at him through the open window. Still feeling mutinous, she pointed her finger at him. "One of these days, Ethan...one of these days you're going to be sorry you wasted all this time arguing with me."

As Ethan watched her walk away, his smile wavered and died. Then he took a deep, weary breath. "Tell me something I don't know," he whispered into the darkness.

"You're late."

Julia kept walking to where Ethan had parked the Cessna, confident that he would fall into step beside her. "Not that I'm talking to you this morning, but I'm two minutes early."

"Well, normally you're fifteen minutes early."

"Worried that I stood you up?"

"Nope," he countered, matching her cheeky smile for cheeky smile, though he wondered what was going on behind the dark lenses of her sunglasses. He dropped his gaze over her outfit. The buttercup shirt and grass-green, bib overalls made her look about seventeen. "Cute," he murmured, giving a tug to the scarf with which she'd tied back her hair. "Mata Hari on Friday night and Rebecca of Sunnybrook Farm on Saturday morning. Who would have guessed what was behind that quiet demeanor?"

"That's right, get my adrenalin flowing and my temper aroused, so I won't miss you while I'm gone."

Grinning, Ethan handed her the Cessna's checklist. "I've just finished filling the tanks and giving it a general inspection."

"Well, you won't mind if I do one of my own, will you?" she drawled, tossing her tote bag into the plane. "I have this instructor who's a real pain about following procedure."

Ethan swept his hand toward the plane, inviting her to the task, but approval warmed his heart as he watched her quickly but expertly do the preflight inspection. He was very proud of her. She could still make him shake his head when she called an aileron a thingamajig, but when it came to safety, he knew he could count on her to obey the rules.

"Now remember, the only difference between this and the short-distance flights you've made is mileage, but we've gone over your maps a dozen times and worked through practically every conceivable problem you might have. As I told you before, I don't expect you to call me when you reach San Antonio, because I know you're going to have a lot on your mind. But don't forget to phone me when you reach Laredo, got it?"

"Yes, Ethan," she groaned, shaking her head. "I'm surprised you're not stowing away on the plane to make sure I follow your directions."

"Believe me, if I thought I could fit and the rules didn't strictly forbid it, I would." He took a step back and tipped his head toward the Cessna. "Well...what are you waiting for?"

A kiss, she thought, her eyes still burning from the tears of frustration and hopelessness she'd shed last night. "I don't suppose it's crossed your mind to wish me luck?"

"It goes without saying, Mouse."

"Most things do with you," she muttered, turning on her heel. Before she could take a step, however, Ethan's big hand came down upon her shoulder, stopping her.

"Julia." Feeling her freeze, wait, he stroked the tense muscles he felt under his thumb. "Good luck, honey."

Impulsively she spun around and rose on tiptoe to kiss him quick and hard. Then she ran to the plane. By the time Ethan recovered, the Cessna was on the runway. As the plane lifted off the ground and climbed, Ethan knew his heart was following.

Two and a half hours later he understood why.

He was working in his hangar—or making a pretense of working. Most of the time he kept watching the clock and estimating how far along she would be.

When the phone rang he grabbed it, smiling, certain that it was Ken in the office, who'd promised to call as soon as he was in touch with San Antonio air traffic control and knew she'd landed and taken off safely.

"What took you?" he said in lieu of a greeting. A moment later his heart stopped.

"Ethan...maybe you'd better come on over here. San Antonio says Julia disappeared from their radar a half hour ago."

Chapter Ten

Ethan raced to the main office, not even remembering if he'd hung up his own phone or simply dropped it. When he burst through the front door, Ken Spivet was taking another call, and the airport's general manager and the other employees were hovering nearby. All of them had one thing in common; their expressions reflected tension and deep concern.

Though Ken raised his hand, signaling him to wait a moment, Ethan immediately demanded, ''Tell me what you know.'' He couldn't, wouldn't speak the question that was at the forefront of his thoughts.

''Ken's on the phone with the San Antonio police right now,'' Dick Stanton, the general manager, told him. ''They've been advised of the area where she disappeared from radar, and they're going to contact local police and sheriff departments out there to ask them to look around. An air patrol helicopter's been sent up, too. Even though it's hilly terrain, a plume of smoke—''

"You're damn quick with your assumptions!" Ethan snapped, taking a step toward the burly man.

"Easy does it," Ken said, hanging up the phone. Looking as formidable as a poplar trying to stake ground between two redwoods, he stepped between them. But his rangy build was deceiving, and he easily pushed both men apart. "No one's saying she's gone down, Ethan, but we have to cover all the possibilities."

"Yeah. Okay, you're right," Ethan muttered, backing off and raking his hands through his hair. Glancing over his shoulder, he shot Dick an apologetic look. "Sorry."

"Forget it. I already have."

Ken took Ethan's arm and led him to one of the maps hanging on the wall. He pointed to an area northwest of San Antonio. "This is where she'd been holding. They'd had a problem earlier in the day, and traffic was still backed up, so they'd asked her to stand by and try again in fifteen or twenty minutes. Fifteen minutes later she asked for an update and was told there was still a backlog. You know how it can be, Ethan."

Frustrating, boring, occasionally unnerving...Ethan knew. "She was intimidated by the San Antonio portion of this trip, what with all the air bases *and* the commercial traffic. That's why I wanted her to get it over with first." He could have sent her to another location, but he'd wanted her to face her fear, because he'd believed it was the only way to defeat it. "Have they continued trying to make radio contact?"

"You know they have," Ken said, though his voice held no rebuke. He gripped Ethan's shoulder. "There's nothing."

"Dear God in heaven." Ethan closed his eyes. Terror clawed at him from the inside and threatened to burst through his chest, his throat. He clenched his hands into fists. Julia...*Julia*. His body shook with the soul-deep cry of her name. What had he done? "I have to use one of your phones," he said, twisting away from Ken as much as from the questions and self-directed accusations that flooded his mind. "Her father needs to be told."

A short time later Woody and Harlan arrived to join the group of grim-faced sentinels pacing in the airport office. Ethan had called his father and asked him to go to the Woods home to break the news. At least, he noted upon seeing how Woody was relying on his father's supportive arm, they seemed to have forgotten their misunderstanding.

Ethan updated them on the situation, and Woody slumped into a nearby chair, dropping his head into his hands. "It's all my fault. If I hadn't tricked her into taking these lessons in the first place, this would never have happened. She never wanted to fly."

"Maybe not before, but her feelings have changed," Ethan told him, keeping his gaze on the plastic foam cup he was meticulously dissecting.

After considering that, Woody nodded his agreement. "She'd mentioned something to that effect. I'd like to believe she meant it."

With even her father slipping into using the past tense when referring to Julia, Ethan found his temper, his sanity, pushed that much closer to the edge. He didn't know how much more he could stand.

Flinging the cup into the trash bin, he went to the window and watched the wind sock across the field flutter in the breeze. Julia was always remarking that it was ridiculous to call it a sock when it resembled a long stocking cap. She enjoyed arguing over the damnedest things.

Where are you?

Was she hurt? Was she frightened? He felt so helpless, so damned impotent. The urge to do violence, to do *something* physical was almost unrestrainable. God, what was he going to do if he lost her?

An hour passed and then another. The phone rang

again and again, and each time Ethan's body went ramrod straight until every muscle was aching as if he'd been through a major workout. Still there was no news about Julia.

Feeling claustrophobia settling upon him, he stepped outside for some fresh air. The late-July sun was sinking toward the west, but still high and hot enough to fry eggs on the sidewalk. Gratefully Ethan lifted his face to it. His chill went bone deep.

Behind him came the sound of the door opening and shutting. He tensed, then relaxed when his father appeared at his side. He wasn't in the mood for company, but his father was hardly that. Theirs might not be a traditional relationship, but the closeness was there. They didn't speak for several minutes, yet Ethan felt the support and was grateful for it.

"I don't think I can take much more of this," he said at last, his voice thick with suppressed emotion.

"Yes, you can. You have to, when there's nothing else to do."

"I should already be on my way up there, helping in the search." Ethan shoved his hands deep into his pockets. "I hate feeling so useless."

Harlan shifted, and beneath his feet pebbles crunched in protest. It sounded abnormally loud in the intermittent silences. "I know. But you're not familiar with the area. It's best you leave the searching to the ones who are." He considered his son's stark, haunted face and purged the air from his lungs. "You've come to care for her a great deal, haven't you?"

"All I can think about is that I didn't tell her I loved her before she left."

"You'll have your chance, son. That old saying about no news being good news has to hold some merit."

"I hope so, Dad. It's all I'm hanging on to."

The office door burst open. "Ethan—phone!" Ken called. "It's some old guy, and he insists on talking to you."

The man's name was Newell Fortenberry or Fountainberry, Ethan couldn't tell which, because of a bad connection. He did make out that he lived on a tiny, out-of-the-way airstrip north of Uvalde.

"Had me a visitor a while ago, and she asked me to give you a call. 'Course, my phone's been out of order for a couple days, so I had to drive twenty miles to my neighbor's place before I could do that."

"Julia—are you saying you spoke to Julia Woods?" Ethan demanded, straining to hear through the static.

"Eh? Julie, yeah. Nice little chicken. Certainly was a surprise to wake up from my siesta and—"

"Is she all right?" Ethan yelled, when the old man's voice disappeared in a swarm of buzzing.

"What—how did she end up near—Uvalde, you say?"

"You want what? Listen, son, we got a bad connection and the battery on my hearing aid is running down, so why don't I talk and you save your questions for her? She figured that you'd be getting worried by now and wanted you to know that she had some trouble, but was on her way back."

"Trouble? What happened?" Ethan shouted.

"Happy? Why, yes, I'd say she was happy. Mind you, it took her a while before she could bring herself to get back in that little bean jumper. But as I told her—see, I flew in the big war, old WW II— I told her when something like that happens, you just gotta do it, before you lose your nerve."

"That's fine, Mr. . . . sir. But—"

"Anytime, son, anytime. You tell her to drop in on old Newly again. You come, too. Gets quiet out our way, what with it being just me and the dogs, know what I mean? Bye now!"

"No! Don't—" The line went dead. Ethan pulled the receiver away from his ear and stared at it in disbelief. "He hung up on me."

"What did he say?" Harlan demanded.

"Julia, you said he talked to Julia?" Woody asked excitedly.

Everyone bombarded him with questions at once, until Ethan had to hold up his hands and demand they give him a moment to make sense of it himself. Then he tried to repeat everything he'd been told. Finally he uttered a weary, incredulous laugh. "Over fourteen million people in this state, and she finds the one character who's hard of hearing and probably gives landing clearances by smoke signal. But the good news is that Julia *is* on her way back."

"Thank God," Woody said over all the shouts and cheers of relief and satisfaction. "But what in the world was she doing near Uvalde?"

"Your guess is as good as mine." Once again, Ethan's expression grew grim and he massaged his stiff neck. "Maybe the trouble that old guy mentioned had to do with her navigational equipment. We'll just have to wait until she can tell us herself. Damn, I wish he'd mentioned what time she took off, so we could estimate her time of arrival. Let's take a look at that map again."

They analyzed, estimated and speculated. It killed all of twelve minutes. The reports to the authorities in San Antonio to call off the phone and ground search took another half hour. After that every minute was an eternity—but not, they were quick to remind each other, the torture it had been before. Finally Julia's weary voice came over the radio, announcing her approach.

A cheer rose in the room. Woody slapped his palm against Harlan's, then dragged a handkerchief out of his pants pocket and blew his nose. Ethan slumped back against a post and, closing his eyes against the unexpected sting of tears, sent up a prayer of thanks.

It was Ken Spivet who picked up the mike and keyed it. "Three Five Alpha, Gator Tower. The strip is yours. Welcome back, stranger."

They rushed out to watch the Cessna land and decided to wait for her at the hangar. By now everyone who hung around the airport with any regularity knew of the daylong drama, and as Julia stepped from the Cessna there was cheering, whistling and applause. Everyone demanded a hug and the details of what had happened. Everyone, that is, except Ethan, who'd retreated to the back of the crowd and had finally settled on the wing of his stunt plane to watch.

It took Julia several moments to spot him. Thereafter she was acutely aware, even wary, her gaze returning to him again and again as she briefly told her story.

"A—a bird... I don't know whether it was a hawk or what, struck me. It was awful and I'm afraid I panicked. I left the San Antonio area and eventually spotted this small airport where I set down. Mr. Fortenberry...Newell, the man I asked to call you, was very kind. He inspected the plane with me and showed me that except for—well, at any rate, the plane was airworthy. I'm sorry for all the trouble and worry I know I caused and—'' once again she sought Ethan in the crowd ''—and for letting you down.''

''Horsefeathers,'' Woody replied, finally stuffing his handkerchief back into his pocket. ''There'll be no more talk like that. The important thing is that you're back and you're all right. What you need now is to go home and get some rest.''

As the idea was seconded and everyone conscientiously began to withdraw, Harlan cleared his throat and pulled his friend aside. ''Uh, Woody... maybe Julia can make other arrangements to get a ride home.''

''Don't be ridiculous. I'm her father. Who else is going to take my little girl if—oomph!'' Suffering an elbow to his ribs, he followed Harlan's nod and saw Julia already walking toward Ethan.

''I think,'' Harlan drawled under his breath, ''you and I should mosey over to Rocky's and have a few cold ones.''

''Maybe even dinner,'' Woody replied, as Ethan pushed away from the stunt plane and took his first step toward her.

''Didn't Rocky say she was having that big-screen TV put in today?''

''Why, I believe you're right.''

"And your favorite Western's going to be on the late show."

"Should we say goodbye?"

"Do you think they'd notice?"

Julia was aware of nothing but the man who filled her range of vision. At her worst moment, she'd wondered if she would ever see him again. Flying home, she'd worried about how disappointed he would be in her. And for the last ten minutes she'd agonized over the way he had been keeping his distance. When they were finally only a foot apart, she discovered that she'd forgotten everything she'd planned to say.

"You look like a breeze would knock you off your feet," he murmured, his gaze sweeping over her face, as if he were in a hurry to restock memory banks.

"Always the quick one with the compliments, aren't you?"

"Give me a few minutes. The world hasn't turned right side out yet."

"Couldn't tell by looking at you."

Ethan smiled faintly, understanding the confusion in her eyes even as he reveled in the adoration he saw there. "That's because you're too busy looking for warts. Why don't you get in the Jeep? I'll collect your tote and take you home."

Not exactly champagne and roses, Julia thought,

doing as he suggested. Not exactly a bone-crushing hug or a heart-melting kiss, either. But interesting. Had that line about the world being inside out been true? He could maintain such a poker face when he wanted to, she thought, watching him coming toward the Jeep.

They'd driven approximately a mile when she decided she couldn't stand another moment of the reverberating silence. "Ethan, say something. If you're going to read me the riot act, I'd just as soon get it over with."

"In a minute."

Exasperated, she rolled down her window and, closing her eyes, tilted her head toward the hot wind. But rather than soothe, it stimulated, so that when they arrived at her house, she grabbed up her tote bag and jumped out. The anger that bubbled within her was welcome after so many hours of weakness and worry.

He had a lot of nerve, treating her like this, she fumed. All she'd wanted was a hug, maybe a word or two of reassurance, understanding.

She didn't know or care if he was following her, but when she heard the kitchen door open and shut again behind her, she knew that was a lie. She wanted the confrontation. A final one. Dropping the tote bag onto a dinette chair she spun around, ready to tell him what she thought of him and how she wanted him to get out—out of her life and out of her heart. Instead she was lifted off the floor and crushed against his pounding heart.

"Never, *never* scare me like that again," Ethan muttered, a second before crushing his mouth to hers.

A weak sound of surprise shot up Julia's throat and her arms wrapped around his neck. She matched him kiss for kiss, demand for demand, and answered his urgent exploration with her own.

Dizzying moments later she threw back her head to gasp for breath. "I was thinking...of taking the stunt plane up tomorrow."

He shifted one hand to the back of her head and drew her close for another bone-melting kiss. This time the sound that broke from Julia was a whimper of pleasure.

"Maybe try my hand at parachuting," she breathed, gazing at his mouth with dreamy eyes.

"Over my dead body."

"Ethan—not that I'm complaining, mind you— but what's going on?"

A slow smile spread over his face. "You haven't figured it out yet?"

All that Julia had figured out was that they were moving, and when she felt her mattress beneath her, she lifted an eyebrow in query. "Maybe you'd better spell things out for me."

Ethan lowered himself beside her and framed her face with his hands. "I'm never going to let you out of my sight again, at least, not without having told you how I feel about you first. I don't care if you're driving to the market or flying to Timbuktu. You're going to know you're the most important part of my life, and that that life wouldn't be worth living if you aren't in it. Every time you leave, you're going to know you're taking my heart with you, so maybe it will make you come back just that much sooner. You're going to know I want you and need you...but most of all you're going to know I love you, Julia Woods."

"Oh, Ethan." Tears flooded Julia's eyes, and she touched his cheek with wonder. "That was the most beautiful thing I've ever heard."

"Don't cry, baby," he groaned, kissing away the droplets that slipped down the side of her face.

"I can't help it. I'd just about convinced myself that I was never going to hear anything close to that from you."

"I know." The memory of his stupidity and fear shadowed his eyes. "Today showed me how foolish I'd been about things."

"So you'll believe me now when I tell you that your bank account isn't what's going to guarantee our happiness, and that I wouldn't love you any better if you were ridiculously rich?"

"I suppose I have to, because I know I can't go on like this." Lifting his head, he gazed down at her. He owed her more, but the power of the emotions churning inside him made him feel so vulnerable. That alone was unsettling.

Julia felt the shudder that passed through him and drew his head to her breast. "Nobody asks for this, Ethan, but it might help you if you knew there's someone equally shaken, equally vulnerable, waiting to share it with you. Me. Tell me what you're thinking."

"There were moments I thought I was going to lose my mind today. I pictured the most awful things. I could see you lying somewhere hurt, bleeding—alone. You didn't even know you'd taken my love with you. I denied you even that." He shifted so that he could bury his face in the shallow valley of her breasts. "God, I was scared."

"I was scared, too," she whispered, combing her fingers through his hair. "When that bird hit, I thought it was all over. It was only when I allowed myself to think of you, remember what being in your arms was like, that I began to regain control and pay attention to where I was and what I had to do. I knew I wanted a chance to come back, to convince you that we belonged together and deserved a chance to make things work."

"You're never going to get an argument from me about that again."

The fervent promise was punctuated with a kiss that was achingly tender. Even as Julia's sigh of pleasure warmed his lips, he slid his hands up to cup her breasts and won himself another kiss.

"Ethan...my father could be home at any moment."

"I have a feeling we won't see either of our fathers for a while. They know we need time to settle things between us," he murmured, slipping the straps of her overalls from her shoulders.

"Settle?" Her voice sounded breathless as he slid them to her waist, then began unbuttoning her blouse. Each inch of skin he exposed was subjected to attentive and thorough exploration.

"A wedding date."

"Ah. No rush. What are you doing tomorrow?"

As she began tugging his T-shirt out of his jeans, he smiled. "We'll also need to plan...on who's moving in with whom."

"Now that could create some problems."

Ethan didn't bother looking up from the pink and mauve beauty he'd exposed. "We'll play dirty and use logic on them...announce we'll need a nursery soon."

"You keep doing that...and we might."

"I'm counting on it." He jerked his T-shirt over

his head and, covering her with his body, stroked her hair with his hands. "We've wasted so much precious time already, sweetheart. I know that financially things might not be easy at first, but—"

"If people always waited until they could afford marriage and children, they never would do either."

Lowering his forehead to hers, he sent up another prayer of thanks. "I'm going to make you happy, love."

"Oh, Ethan, you already have."

"Uh-uh." A wicked gleam lighted his eyes. "It gets better."

Soft laughter bubbled up into Julia's throat. She combed her fingers through the wild tangle of his hair and drew him nearer. "Prove it."

Epilogue

A baby's cry drowned the clanging of swords in the swashbuckler playing on TV. Without taking his eyes off the screen, Harlan nudged Woody.

"That's yours."

"How can you tell?"

"Higher voice. It's yours."

Putting his bowl of popcorn onto the coffee table, Woody rose from the sofa and hurried down the hall to the bedroom, where two babies lay on a full-size bed, framed by a half-dozen pillows. The one on the right had kicked off her blanket and lifted feet clad in pink knit booties in demand when she spotted him.

"Shh. Hey, pumpkin," Woody cooed, as he bent

to lift her into his arms. "We don't want to wake up your brother. Is Grampa's best girl ready for her din-din?" Just as he started down the hall, another cry sounded. He hurried into the living room.

"Here," he said, passing the infant to Harlan. "Take Lisa. I have to go back for Randy."

"On your way past the kitchen bring me a beer."

"I've only got two hands, Harlan, and the kids want their bottles. Get your beer yourself."

Sighing, Harlan rose, and with Lisa in his arms, went to the kitchen, where he tested the water warming the babies' bottles. After shutting off the flame beneath the pot, he shuffled to the refrigerator to get a bottle of beer. "We must have been crazy to encourage Ethan and Julia to spend the night in Houston," he said, as Woody joined him in the kitchen, holding their grandson in his arms.

"Well, things have been hectic for them these past four months, what with the babies being born and the business growing faster than they'd expected. This trip to pick up that second plane was just the opportunity they needed to spend a little time alone."

"What am I talking to you for?" Harlan grumbled. He glanced down to wiggle his bushy eyebrows at his granddaughter. "You're the one who got us into this mess in the first place."

Snatching the beer out of his hand and replacing

it with a bottle of formula, Woody nudged Harlan back into the living room. "Stop complaining, and look at the bright side for once. You don't have to eat Ethan's cooking anymore, do you?"

"No, now I get to listen to your snoring all night."

"Shut your door if you don't like it."

"It doesn't help!"

They sat down on the sofa and, ignoring each other, began feeding their grandchildren. Soon the gluttonous, suckling sounds had Woody making silly faces at Randy and Harlan whispering baby talk to Lisa.

"I guess they're kinda cute," Harlan said after a while. "But they'll be more fun to be around when they're old enough to talk and stuff."

"Yeah. I'm looking forward to when we can take them fishing."

"I saw an ad in the paper for swing sets. We should get one for the backyard. We'll save a few bucks if we put it together ourself."

"We. Ha! The first minute you get confused by the instructions, you'll leave the mess for me to figure out."

"Will not."

"Will, too. What about that clothes dryer outside? If it wasn't for me— What's wrong?" Woody asked, seeing Harlan sniff and grimace.

"Uh, Woody. Here. You were supposed to be taking care of Lisa, weren't you?"

"Nope. Forget it."

"It's your turn. I got stuck with changing both of them last time, when you were at the grocery store, and you agreed you owed me one."

"I paid you back the following week."

"You did not!"

"Well, stop yelling, or you'll give the kids indigestion." Woody slid nearer and switched babies with Harlan.

As he started down the hall, Harlan winked at his grandson and called over his shoulder. "Yep, Woody. This sure is a fine arrangement we've gotten ourselves into."

"Oh, shut up, Harl."

The Beechcraft lifted away from Gator Cove Municipal Airport, and Julia's expression was pensive as she looked out the passenger window. "Ethan, are you sure this is a good idea? Spending an entire night away from the children? I know we already made the hotel reservations, but Houston isn't exactly around the corner."

"Spoken just like a mother leaving her babies for the first time," he teased before sending her a tender smile. "Stop worrying, love. They're going to be fine. Why don't you sit back and daydream about the Jacuzzi we're going to settle into after we sign the papers for the new plane.''

For the first time since they'd dropped off the children with their fathers, Julia's smile came naturally. Ethan sounded more excited about the prospect of a romantic evening with just the two of them than about picking up their second Beechcraft for Ross Aviation. But that made him all the dearer to her.

She was so proud of him. In the fourteen months since their wedding he'd really proved himself. As a result, the business was not only acquiring its second plane, but he'd just hired a new pilot who would start next week. Julia knew he would insist she'd been instrumental in the company's success, as well, since she maintained the books while continuing her job at city hall. It was Ethan's talent as a pilot and businessman, however, that had translated into growth for the company and Gator Cove.

''The Jacuzzi sounds heavenly, but to tell you the truth, I wouldn't care if it was our bathtub at home, as long as we're in it together.''

''Uh, wait until we're a little higher before you tempt me to put this thing on automatic pilot, will you, sweetheart?''

That made Julia glance outside again, and she frowned when she realized they weren't making their usual climb for a long-distance flight. ''Ethan, what are you doing?'' she asked, when he also turned in the direction opposite to the one she'd expected.

"Oh, just following through on a little impulse." He glanced out his own window to judge their location, and as they began flying over the community's most prestigious neighborhood, he picked up the paper bag he'd hidden beneath his seat.

Julia's eyes widened in disbelief when he opened the side window, lifted the handful of rubber alligators from the bag and tossed them out. "Ethan!" She swung around in her seat and watched several of the creatures hit Mayor Bainbridge's swimming pool. "Oh, no! He's going to know exactly who did that."

"I hope so." Ethan chuckled. "I might be a successful businessman now, but I don't want anyone to think I've changed completely."

"No threat of that." Julia laughed, shaking her head. Releasing her seat belt just for a moment, she leaned over and gave her husband a kiss on his cheek. "I love you, you crazy man."

His eyes twinkled with mischief. "Prove it."

"At this altitude? You'll wait for the Jacuzzi and be glad of it."

Giving a lusty, rebel yell, Ethan turned toward Houston, and the Beechcraft rose eagerly into the bright, summer sky.

* * * * *

SPECIAL EDITION

Stories of love and life, these powerful
novels are tales that you can identify with—
romances with "something special" added
in!

Fall in love with the stories of authors such
as **Nora Roberts, Diana Palmer, Ginna Gray**
and many more of your special favorites—as
well as wonderful new voices!

Special Edition brings you
entertainment for the heart!

SILHOUETTE® *Desire*®

Do you want...

Dangerously handsome heroes

Evocative, everlasting love stories

Sizzling and tantalizing sensuality

Incredibly sexy miniseries like **MAN OF THE MONTH**

Red-hot romance

Enticing entertainment that can't be beat!

You'll find all of this, and much *more* each and every month in **SILHOUETTE DESIRE**. Don't miss these unforgettable love stories by some of romance's hottest authors. Silhouette Desire—where your fantasies will always come true....

If you've got the time...
We've got the
INTIMATE MOMENTS

Passion. Suspense. Desire. Drama. Enter a world that's larger than life, where men and women overcome life's greatest odds for the ultimate prize: love. Nonstop excitement is closer than you think...in Silhouette Intimate Moments!

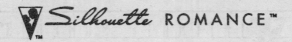
Silhouette ROMANCE™

What's a single dad to do when he needs a wife by next Thursday?

Who's a confirmed bachelor to call when he finds a baby on his doorstep?

How does a plain Jane in love with her gorgeous boss get him to notice her?

From classic love stories to romantic comedies to emotional heart tuggers, **Silhouette Romance** offers six irresistible novels every month by some of your favorite authors! Such as...beloved bestsellers **Diana Palmer, Annette Broadrick, Suzanne Carey, Elizabeth August** and **Marie Ferrarella,** to name just a few—and some sure to become favorites!

Fabulous Fathers...Bundles of Joy...Miniseries... Months of blushing brides and convenient weddings... Holiday celebrations... You'll find all this and much more in **Silhouette Romance**—always emotional, always enjoyable, always about love!